Touched by Death

a ForbiddenFiction Special Collection
edited by D.M. Atkins

I0539882

ForbiddenFiction
www.forbiddenfiction.com

an imprint of

Fantastic Fiction Publishing
www.fantasticfictionpublishing.com

TOUCHED BY DEATH
A Forbidden Fiction book

Fantastic Fiction Publishing
Hayward, California

© D.M. Atkins, 2012
Individual stories © by their authors.

All rights reserved. No part of this work may be used or reproduced in any manner whatsoever without permission from the publisher, except as allowed by fair use. For more information, contact publisher@forbiddenfiction.com.

CREDITS
Anthology Editor: D.M. Atkins
Story Editors: D.M. Atkins, Rylan Hunter, Lon Sarver
Cover and interior illustrations design: D.M. Atkins, Siolnatine
Art and photographs: Creatista , eddiephotograph, feedough, foqus, GNBDesigns, is2, jeancliclac, kovalvs, macky_ch, Natlit, Pat Durkin, Sandralise, Spectral, Wavebreak Media at Pixmac; Anneka, Chu-x, FXQuadro at Shutterstock, Soupstudio at Dreamstime; Hamed Saber (back cover)
Production Editor: Erika L Firanc
Proofreading: Arcanox, Fireffly, JhP323, Kailin Morgan, Star-Damaged, Todd Michaels

SKU: SPC-000001-02 FFP
ISBN: 978-1-62234-082-8

Published in the United States of America

Joey, despite being dead, is a very good-looking ghost...

... with his shaggy brown hair, big hazel eyes, and the tongue stud that Grant is sure can't actually be there. Sometimes, Grant has dreams where Joey is corporeal, and they somehow get into situations he wouldn't mind acting out if only it were real. But it's stupid and pointless and crazy, so Grant does his best not to think of Joey like that.

Joey never seems to notice the way Grant stares at his mouth, the curve of his jaw as he thinks about drawing it in one of the notebooks he's tried to keep hidden under his bed. Joey just sighs at the coffee and sweeps his transparent hand through the countertop..

"Can you see other ghosts?" Grant asks as he leaves the kitchen for his studio.

He used to think it was weird, having gotten the apartment so he could live alone and work on his art, only to find Joey and, clearly, Joey wasn't going anywhere — Grant hasn't asked about that yet either. He's not sure if he's scared to know or if it really doesn't matter. Joey never says anything.

Joey drifts after him lazily, ruffling his hair, and Grant looks away, because, like everything else with Joey, he has nice hair too.

"I've never seen any others," Joey replies vaguely. "But I don't really leave the apartment."

Also recommended...

You may also enjoy this other special collection:

Wicked Fairy Tales, A ForbiddenFiction Special Collection
http://forbiddenfiction.com/library/collection/SPC-1.100002

An anthology of bedtime stories that are definitely not for children.

Just what kind of happy goes into "happily ever after?" As children, it was enough that Pinocchio got to be a real boy and that Red wasn't eaten by the wolf. As adults, we have a slightly different perspective. Being a real boy means having boy parts, and being eaten by someone big and bad doesn't mean quite the same thing it once did.

Ever wonder what mermaids do with the swimmers they seduce? Or why a dragon might prefer a castle-guarded princess to a nice, easy field of sheep? What if your fairy godmother wasn't circumspect in what wishes could be granted, or if that dainty little fairy had a much bigger appetite than one might guess?

DISCLAIMER

This book is a work of fiction which contains explicit erotic content; it is intended for mature readers. Do not read this if it's not legal for you.

All the characters, locations and events herein are fictional. While elements of existing locations or historical characters or events may be used fictitiously, any resemblance to actual people, places or events is coincidental. Real, historic personalities appearing are not meant to be accurate representations, but adapted characters for the dramatic purposes of this fictitious universe. Also, while we have taken great care to be as accurate as possible in many details regarding the period, some details were deliberately changed to fit the story.

This story is not intended to be used as an instruction manual. It may contain descriptions of erotic acts that are immoral, illegal, or unsafe. Do not take the events in this story as proof of the plausibility or safety of any particular practice.

If you enjoy this collection, you can sign up for a free membership at ForbiddenFiction.com and discuss it with other readers and the authors at the *Touched by Death Special Collection* story page at http://forbiddenfiction.com/library/collection/SPC-1.100001

We do our best to proof all our work, but if you spot a text error we missed, please let us know via our website Contact Form at http://forbiddenfiction.com/Contact

To all our beloved dead.

Contents

Raven and Crow

Luna Lawrence

When Angelina Grimke meets Edgar Allan Poe at a séance, he mocks her attempts to contact her dead fiancé, but hints that he knows a "scientific" way to raise the dead. Tormented by her grief for her lost love, she seeks out Poe who proposes to use "electro-magnetism" to bring her lover back. Can passion raise the dead?

1

Raven and Crow

I hadn't the imagination to be as rude as I wished to the young man facing me. Yet I tried, and immediately felt guilty.

"Thy attack on our efforts to reach the blessed dead is unwarranted, sir."

His dark eyes seemed to glow in satisfaction over his droopy, petulant mouth. He'd provoked me just as he wished. And I had responded not as I wished.

At that moment our hostess intervened, calling us to leave her overheated parlor and sit about the dining table. I was glad to be seated by the elderly doctor, and thus not required to touch the delicate hands of my persecutor. He, meanwhile, continued to stare brazenly at me. I tried to deny my imagination of his thoughts, how he must see me as gawky and odd, horse-faced and lank-haired. But I treasured my lack of vanity and wished to flaunt my plainness and my simple dress as if they had been the gaudiest of jewels.

Pride! I stamped at the serpent in my heart with all the fury I felt for the young man and his ornate cravat. He looked now at our hostess with an undeniable sneer, as she rose to admit our principal guest. But the young man did not turn his head toward the shape moving slowly into the dim room, addressing me again, instead.

"You are from Charleston, are you not, Miss Grimke? Surely slaves nourished you, protected you, and sustained you in your infant days. You are the true efflorescence of that civilization. Surely you were taught their...superstitious...practices from birth, so you must pardon the ignorance of we who had the misfortune to be educated in the ways of scientific endeavor."

My sister Sarah gasped at his effrontery from her seat beside him.

"I beg thy pardon, sir, but we have left that benighted area, and find in the cruel practice of slavery no cause for jocularity. We follow the cause of Abolition." Although she spoke severely, he listened with a smile that continued to play on his pretty little mouth.

"And Abolition has given you wisdom beyond reason, has it not?" He spoke in a contemptuous tone, arching a fine brow under the artfully tousled curls on his forehead.

Someone who was a man and not given to the pacific ways of the Friends might have struck him at that moment.

Being a Quaker woman, I bit my lip in irritation and struggled with my anger. This was no mood for our enterprise tonight. I left his taunts unanswered and attempted to meditate on the dear face of Edward. But alas, I could conjure only the wretched grimace of his deathbed now, never that fair and gentle countenance that had so often welcomed me in sweet silence in the Frosts' parlor.

Mrs. Frost now led her guest to the head of the table, next to my own place. A sort of sweet mustiness arose toward me from the dark veil that swathed the head of the dumb figure as it settled in the chair, and I could not help but shudder at the thought of touching the ungloved hand that stretched out toward me. A sepulchral voice rose from within the veil, deep as a man's.

"Let us clasp hands," it intoned.

The young man across the table snorted, and my eye flashed toward him. He dropped his head in a parody of reverence, and I lay my lace-mitted paw lightly on the ham-like fist of Dr. McNevers while Sarah clutched my other fingers tightly in her own. Her fear shot through me like a bee-sting: were we about to invoke the powers of the angels or the Devil? Were we parting a veil the Almighty had drawn for good reason? Her beliefs were still so much what she'd learned from the Friends – and her fears, too.

Her fears were never mine. What we can see, what we can do – we should. The Lord who gave us the will and courage to act meant that we should do so. I squeezed her fingers in comfort, but knew I sent her only confirmation of my ungovernable boldness. She distrusted Mr. Swedenborg's teachings, but to me they offered both the hope of seeing my beloved again and the opening of the door to unimaginable mysteries. What might we learn in this ordinary Philadelphia parlor, the eight of us seated at Mrs. Frost's mahogany table with its lace cloth?

The young man across the table, however, seemed barely able to suppress his amusement.

The veiled figure began to chant in some unknown argot, and then drew a sharp breath. The lamplight wavered. A cold wind brushed my face.

A moan rose from the veiled one.

Edward, I called in my heart, Edward, come! Touch me again! Even cold from the grave, even fluorescent with decay, your hand on my face again would be life to me. I squeezed the hands I held and prayed as the moaning swelled to fill the room. Surely Edward was coming, coming to hold me as he never had in life!

"Nevermore," was the sepulchral tone that swelled in the silence. "Nev...er...mooore."

I dared to part my eyes, hoping for a glimpse of Edward, however eaten by worms he might be, still an angel's countenance to me.

My eyes met the sardonic gaze of the infidel across from me. The young man at that moment lost all control and let out a choking guffaw.

"I beg pardon," he gasped, and fled the table.

The hands he'd been holding fell against the table like cold fish flopping on the shore.

As had happened to me since childhood, my rage rose up against my better nature and forced me to my feet. Unheeding of the cries from Sarah and the others, I pushed blindly past them and out the door behind him.

I rushed through the empty dark hall where he must have gone and threw open the outer door. He stood on the little stoop, bent over to pet a grey cat that arched and rubbed against his leg. The innocence of his pose did nothing to mollify my rage, especially when he stood and revealed the flask of liquor in his other hand.

One eyebrow arched as he leaned against the icy railing and watched me storm, heedless of the blowing snow and the loop of hair coming undone at the back of my head.

"I would address thee in brotherly love, but I feel none of it," I cried. "Thee may believe or not as is thy wont, but why must thee disturb the endeavors of the faithful to find our loved ones from beyond the grave? If thee had known the pain of such a loss, thee would not be so cruel."

The lamplight from the street gleamed on his broad brow, but under it the eyes were hidden in a darkness that seemed like that of the pit. Had I met the very devil, my rage could not have burned with a fire more bold or less pitying. All the gentleness of my recent teachings cast aside, I longed for a flaming sword to smite him, or at least a tongue with brilliance to cut his smirking pride.

He answered me with silence.

I continued to berate him. As I had lost my Quaker patience, I left off my Quaker speech.

"What could a dandy like you know of the love that lives beyond the grave? You have your drunken revels, your gambling, your harlots…yes, I am from Charleston, Mr. Poe. I know of you as you know of me. Your debts and your quarrels and your dissipation are legend in the city, even now, even to one like me who cares nothing for idle gossip."

The bottomless eyes seemed to glow with dark fire.

"And you knew love, did you, Miss Grimke? Your angelic betrothed showed you its pleasure in full?"

I drew back my hand to strike him in indignation, but stopped short.

A tear glinted in the corner of his eye. In spite of myself, I felt a pang of sympathy. Had even this dissolute monster known the soothing angel of love? Had he his own cherished vision, torn from him by the hand of death?

I thought he would confess his loss, but he turned away from me toward the great moon, gold and heavy in the autumn sky. His voice seemed to come from a distance.

"Forget these charlatans, Miss Grimke. These grotesque mystics have no power like science. With the guidance of the lamp of enlightened reason, I can lead you to the gates of life and death. And you will not need to pay me."

"Science, sir? Science will open the gates that love and prayer find closed?"

"Love and prayer? Can you close the door behind you with a prayer, or open the gate to the street with all your love?"

"No," I admitted, "but neither can you open the tomb with an iron key. Or you may open it, but you will find only the body, not the cherished soul."

His high-pitched laughter chilled me as the veiled figure inside had never done.

"The soul! The soul! I will not promise that, but is the soul really what you long for?"

I shrank from the vile little man and his intrusions into my heart.

And yet it was true. I remembered how my breath had come faster when Edward touched my hand, even though we both wore gloves. I had felt my lips warm and tingling as he looked at me, felt a deeper thrill through the core of my body at the sight of his broad back as he walked down the lane. Now the misery of his deathbed was fading, replaced by a memory I could not speak of, even to Sarah. And this horrid man somehow knew my inmost feelings.

I had left my toleration for arrogant men behind me in the South.

"I long to be out of your company, sir," I said, and turned to walk back into the house.

But during the long hours of the night, his promise kept me wakeful in the shadowed room, my heart thumping as I thought of what he had said. In truth, I had been disappointed, as the evening wore on, by the veiled figure Mrs. Frost had invited—much incomprehensible moaning and murmuring had come from the hidden mouth, but nothing that spoke of Edward. And now, as the window panes turned grey, I told myself again that I was a fool. Death was final, only with God would we ever see the departed again, and that was the end of it. The posers and pretenders who offered to speak with the dead—they had nothing true to offer, but only preyed on our sorrow for their own gain, and I would have nothing more to do with them.

I determined to force myself to work now only for good and so no longer dwell on my loss. To that end, I arose with the sun and soon was at the market, buying food to provide for the few surviving victims of the terrible cholera that had taken Edward. But as I selected the bread that might sustain them, my mind was still on the terrible Mr. Poe.

At Meeting that Sabbath, I found myself still imagining that what he had said might be true. And on the next day, as I helped Sarah prepare a letter to the clergy at home, I found that my grief had crystallized around the words I had heard that evening.

Finally, on Tuesday, I determined to settle the matter. I am not one to dither and mope in silence. This is a task to be completed, I told myself, and set out with no word to Sarah to search for the grim proponent of communication with the hereafter. Mr. Poe lived in Baltimore, that I knew, but Mrs. Frost had told me he was visiting a friend in Germantown. As he was well-known, it took little effort to obtain direction to his friend's habitation.

The house loomed over me and I feared to rub my clothes against its sooty walls, but even more feared to stand on such a desolate street, so I knocked on the peeling door.

Mr. Poe stood before me in a stupor, it seemed, though whether of liquor or sleep I could not say, but I pressed on.

"May I enter, sir? I have come to ask about your experiments."

I held my head high and stepped uninvited through the door, into the very dismal hallway, where the fumes of alcohol arising from my host assaulted my nose and my lungs like the sulphur of hell. My father had often served brandy, in my youth, and I had cared for many a drunkard, making me all too aware of the stumbling and foolishness that might follow.

Yet Mr. Poe, in spite of his bleary eyes and stained shirt, bore himself like a soldier and spoke like a lawyer.

"Pray do enter, Miss Grimke, since you already have done so," he said, lighting a very dim lamp. "Let us sit in the parlor."

Following him into a room that scarce seemed to merit the name, I almost tripped on the teetering piles of books and made my way around a box filled with strange metallic instruments. Under the baleful gaze of some darkly painted Sybil, hung in the gloom at the light's edge, I perched myself on the edge of a threadbare sofa. I shuddered inwardly and cursed myself for coming—nothing in this room could possibly lead me to the light that held Edward.

And yet I had come this far. I spoke as calmly as I could.

"Mr. Poe, you say that science can reach the dead. And that you will show me those wonders. Here I am, then, prepared to be shown."

His heavy lids lifted and the green eyes met mine.

"Indeed, Miss Grimke. I believe that science has that power."

"And how must we proceed?"

I had horrible visions of some chemical mixture poured down my resisting throat, but I kept a steady voice.

Mr. Poe walked to the fireplace and stirred the coals, bringing at least the memory of heat and light into the room. I waited for no invitation, since none seemed forthcoming, but spoke as if to continue our previous conversation.

"Well, then, sir, let us begin."

Mr. Poe turned toward me and opened his bleary eyes a little wider.

"If you want the life, Miss Grimke, you must have the body. We must go to the grave of the one you see to call. The body is the life. As you know."

I believed no such nonsense. Even when I part company with the Society of Friends, I know that my life is my immortal soul. But I had not come to this weird man to debate theology.

"I was not allowed to attend the funeral of this person, Mr. Poe, because my beliefs offended his relations. I would not be welcome at his grave."

I cast my eyes down in sadness, although the thought of meeting Edward's haughty mother and overbearing father with the disreputable Mr. Poe almost brought a smile to my lips, for Edward himself would have laughed long and hard at such an improbable scene.

"Why do you laugh, Miss Grimke? If you doubt me—please, I will detain you no longer."

"Not you, Mr. Poe. I laugh with regret at an old memory—a memory of being cast out and helpless."

"If you are weakened by such treatment, then too should you question this endeavor. Only the cold eye of science can look through the doors of life and death without being driven toward madness."

The afternoon light that had come through the dingy window had begun to wane, so late was the hour and the season. Night approached and his voice darkened. "We will find the grave, Miss Grimke. I know those who work with the dead and they will lead us to it. But you must think what you will find."

"Indeed, Mr. Poe, I want only to hear the voice of one who is gone, to know once more the tender effulgence of that gentle spirit."

Exasperation was evident in the bulging brow, the mouth pursing under the baleful eyes.

"You will not find what you seek, Miss Grimke. Here, I will tell you exactly what will happen. Have you heard of mesmerism? The science of animal magnetism?"

"Something of it—a fluid that makes frog legs jump, is that it?" I had no idea why he suddenly followed this wild tack, but humored him in my hope to obtain my goal.

"Fluid, yes!" His eyes were suddenly blazing with light, his voice fevered. "But, no frogs, no. It is the magnetic currents within us that bear the secret of life. And I—I have learned how to work these currents, how to steer the streams that flow within us! It is the breath of the future—the electrical current! "Listen: several years ago, I saw a man hover between life and death, and I was taught how the passage of current through a wire from my hand to his body created an electric sympathy that allowed me to hold him in stasis, just in the balance between this life and the next. Since then, I have worked—day and night I have worked—so that now I can find the subtlest of currents in a body where the life seems long fled. I have spoken with those long since departed, those who have lain hours or even days with all life seemingly gone."

Despair filled me.

"But this one has been dead for weeks, Mr. Poe. At least two weeks. And he died a dreadful death, of cholera. I think he must have passed long since beyond the reach of your science."

He paced excitedly, his eyes darting to and fro, and the glimmer of the firelight cast him in a ghastly light.

"Perhaps so, perhaps so! But—perhaps not! Let us try, let us try it now."

I felt a cold hand at my heart. Surely it was wrong, sinful and selfish, to call Edward back now that he had passed beyond the threshold of suffering. And yet—just one farewell, I thought, and I will let him go. Just one parting word and I can rest.

I stood.

"Let us go then, Mr. Poe."

The graveyard at twilight was as dismal as it should have been: shadows looming, black birds in withered branches, a distant bell tolling. I had sensibly brought a lantern, but that was my only act of reason. I left while Sarah napped, leaving her a note only that I would return. I slipped down the rough cobbles of the streets alone, meeting insolent stares from more than one rough fellow—but none so rough as the one I went to meet.

My lantern showed him leaning against a stone, a pack slung over his shoulder. He offered no greeting, only a surly gesture of his head toward an ornate crypt in the deeper darkness at the back of the graveyard, sheltered under even darker trees.

I followed him. He walked through the leaning stones with a jerking step, leaving me to trail him like a servant, but his promise burned deeper than my indignation. When he reached the door of the crypt, he leaned heavily against it. The grating of metal on stone irritated me, and I raised my lantern high to see where he led me.

I am no stranger to darkness and squalor. I have been in many dismal places—even in the poorest of slave cabins, in the fusty sick-rooms of the desperate poor, and have sat with death at midnight. But in all those places, my faith guarded my heart.

Entering that door, I left faith behind.

Mr. Poe set down his pack. He drew from it another candle, which he lit, and bade me sit on a stone bench facing the tomb. With tremendous effort he slid the cover off the tomb. The grating of metal against metal made an eldritch screeching, but I sat still as a monument.

I moved to look into the grave.

Edward.

But not as I ever wanted to see him, already putrid with decay. His face, formerly so angelic in its lineaments, sagged and drooped, a sodden, misshapen mass. The once-delicate skin now was blackened and peeled away, showing the bone of his cheek and the rotted flesh. His lips, that once kissed my own so tenderly, were withered and pulled away from his elongated teeth. Horrible to behold! And the odor that arose brought heaves to my stomach. I drew back in disgust, but Mr. Poe clutched at my hand. "Now!" He hissed. "Now we must do it. I have the technique, the instruments, and in you the sympathetic electricity."

He held my hand tightly for a moment, and then opened his pack, removing a disordered mass of strange wires and odd shapes of metal. Moving with agonizing slowness, he disentangled one of the wires and drew it into the tomb, laying a small metal tablet upon the poor face of my beloved. And then Mr. Poe again took my hand and drew me towards him, towards the reeking tomb.

I wanted nothing less than to see movement in that wretched body. I struggled against Mr. Poe.

"No, no. Now is the time!" Mr. Poe continued to pull urgently at my waist, and even lower.

I raised my free hand to push at him, but he caught and held me. I felt the fire of his anger and my own rose to meet it.

With rage I pushed against him, my face inches from his.

And then my body was against his, and I felt the beating of a force that seemed to lift me up and toss me.

Edward lay forgot as Mr. Poe and I grappled against each other, hatred and desire fusing with a power I had never felt. The heat of his body turned my limbs to liquid—I poured against him like boiling mercury. And at the same time I was retching with repulsion at the horror of what he had tried to do, at the stale brandy fumes that clung to him.

I tried to pull away and meet his eye, but his mouth fell on mine. God help me, I sucked at his mouth like a starved person falling on food. My whole body burned and I could scarce know where he touched me and where I touched him.

I tore my bodice open and his wet mouth pulled at my breast. He raised my skirts and caressed my hips, and I ground them against him in wanton fury. He opened his pants. I felt the heat of his bare skin against mine. Something hot and hard pushed against my unclothed body.

I knew what was touching me—I had seen animals enough. Disgust and fire mingled in me, but he was beyond stopping. He thrust his naked organ against my bared stomach. And then lower, towards my parted legs, which I could not bring myself to close. And then he paused, fumbling with one hand at something beside me. I was so besotted with lust that I could not bear his touch to leave me—I reached down to touch that hard organ, felt it throb in my hand. I pulled him back toward me, wanting him to push it into the heat between my legs, where I felt a wetness I had never known.

Instead, his hot hand went beneath me, and he cupped my buttock, pulling it to one side. In the midst of the heat, I felt cold metal, first against my flesh, then sliding between my cheeks to that dark opening. I jerked and almost pulled away, my lust cooled by fear and disgust.

But he caressed me slowly with his other hand, gently parting the flesh between my legs, softly opening it with his fingers. And the heat unfurled inside me again.

He slid his long hot member into the wetness, and my body rose to grind itself against him. Waves of indescribable pleasure coursed through my aching body.

I opened my eyes and then I saw him at last—Edward, a burning light in the darkness behind the head lowered to my bared breasts. The horrible head was drooping to one side, and the rotted eyes tried to open. More skin pulled away as Edward's reanimated corpse tried to move, to rise from the darkness of death.

Mr. Poe took my gasp of horror and despair for passion, and clutched my hips even more tightly, driving himself deeply into my opened body, and I pulled him into me, even as I watched Edward struggle from the grave.

The bones of Edward's hands showed through his flesh when he pulled against the sides of the crypt, trying to drag himself to standing. His poor body was too weak, and the same act that animated him caused him to draw back with revulsion. I could see that the horrible mouth tried to open, to call, and the head lolled on the unsteady shoulders. I wanted to reach out towards him, to call his name—and yet the burning rod pounded between my legs, and I could do nothing but moan. I felt Poe's body rub against the nub of flesh where the pleasure was sharpest, and his fingers, reaching from under my buttocks, rubbed the back entrance where he still held the metal inside me. The heat and motion dragged me toward an ecstasy I could never have imagined, and then I felt a fierce throbbing at the pit of my being.

As my body convulsed in horrid, delicious tremors, Edward's face sagged in horror. He flailed at the air, and with inhuman effort, dragged his body from the tomb. Even as my body throbbed in pleasure and release, I felt the horror of Edward's touch.

Edward moaned, his cold hand grasping my bare leg, but Poe was coming to a shuddering crisis and took no notice. I felt the slime of the grave freezing cold on my hot flesh—just as Poe's thick member spurted hot inside me.

Edward—Poe—I could not tell whether I felt ecstasy or repulsion, but somewhere deep within my body was like a volcano gushing lava. My mind was chaos.

I jerked away, and at that moment, the little metal plug came out of my body. The current broke, and with it, the life that had moved Edward. His body fell lifeless backwards into the tomb, just as Mr. Poe's once-hard member shriveled and withdrew damply from my body.

He turned finally toward the open tomb, where Edward's body lay sprawled in stinking death, again. Poe turned to me with a wild look of triumph, but I was in no mind to attend to him. I drew my clothes over me and stood, shaking but firm on my feet. Lifting my head, I strode from the place.

Mr. Poe followed me. "We have achieved the great goal! We have created the magnetism that reaches into the tomb! Dear lady, your fire has brought the dead to life!"

I laughed a laugh that was not even bitter. "We have raised him and killed him again. Mr. Poe, I have done with your experiments."

And with that I left him standing in the mists of the graveyard, and walked back into the land of the living.

If you enjoyed this story, you can discuss it with other readers and the author at the *Raven and Crow* story page at
http://forbiddenfiction.com/library/story/LL1-1.000022.

The Band Plays On

Theda Black

They met two months ago in an L.A. club—lead guitarist Slater was drowning in a toilet at two in the morning after a ninety minute set and too much liquor and blow. Jonah fished him out. Jonah wasn't into guys, but Slater was the exception to everything.

The Band Plays On

Jonah Everhart didn't fuck guys, and guys didn't fuck him. He liked guys, just not that way.

Then along came Slater. They'd met two months ago in L.A.—Slater was at the Toxicity Club, busy drowning in a toilet at two in the morning after a ninety minute set and too much liquor and blow. Jonah had fished him out.

Slater was front man and founder of the Head Dogs. After a decade of hitting the local venues, touring and summer festivals, the band had finally been approached by an A&R rep looking to sign them for their record label. It'd been party time *all* the time after that, with Jonah along for the ride.

Slater was intelligent and talented, so wasted, led by his dick and his drugs and his never-ending longing for a lost love back in New Orleans. All of it excuses, maybe, to live the way he did. But who was Jonah to judge? He got where Slater was coming from.

Actually, Jonah was pretty sure he loved Slater in an unhealthy suicide pact kind of way.

Jonah loved women, too. He loved talking to them, understood the way they thought. He just couldn't live up to what they wanted. He couldn't live up to what he wanted for himself, either. He was a proud, cock upstanding member of the fuck-yourself-up-and-die club with Slater right there beside him, trying to take the crown away.

But women: he loved to fuck them and be fucked by them, loved their breasts bobbing in his face when they moved, sweet soft skin. He loved to sink inside them, to feel them spasm around him and grip him tight. He loved spreading their legs wide and tasting them, smelling their musk, getting wet from nose to chin, hearing their moans.

He loved lapping at their clits until they screamed, sucking them and then burrowing inside, pointing his tongue and fucking them with it. Loved to make them come, screaming and pulling his hair while they did. Loved it all.

He loved Kylena more than all of them, even though she'd left him after three years of living together. It burned a hole in his gut. He applied liberal amounts of alcohol, pills, you name it—anything to numb the pain. The effect was immediate, though it only made the hole burn more later.

It wasn't like he'd really expected she'd stay with him—there was no way he wouldn't fuck it up. And fuck it up he did, same as with every relationship.

But. At least the world was full of women.

And yet, incredibly, here he was on his back on Slater's shitty sheetless mattress with Slater's dick up his ass. Talk about burning holes.

"Remember that threesome you refused me on at Dante's party? With uh—shit, what's her name—fuck it, it isn't important. The point is the threesome *wasn't* the point. I had an ulterior motive. Wanted to see your dick, man," Slater said. "Make sure you measure up, you know?"

Jonah raised a brow. "You're a cock snob? Huh." He drove his hips up. The burn spread and smoothed out, something good just beneath it. "Surprised you didn't just ask if you wanted a look."

Slater grunted, sinking further inside Jonah's ass. "Knew you'd freak out. Prudence Everhart couldn't wrap his head around a threesome, now could he?"

"Bitch. To think I was played," Jonah said dryly. "And now you've got me. I'll never be able to turn back once I've had a taste of the beast. Is that the idea?" Slater dug his feet into the mattress and shoved his dick deep in response. He hit just right, and Jonah groaned, his cock spurting a little precome onto his stomach.

"Sarcasm is the sign of a weak intellect or some such bullshit, and if you think you can shrivel my manhood with mere words you are talking to the wrong cock," Slater panted. He brushed his lips over Jonah's.

Jonah turned away. "Whoa, cowboy. I did not agree to kiss. That's like what, the Final Frontier or something."

"You didn't say I could fuck you either, but—" Slater pointed out, and Jonah finished with him, "—here we are."

"You keep notching the bedpost, don't you?" added Jonah.

Slater grabbed Jonah's dick and squeezed, shooting him a scornful look. Jonah moaned, twisted in his grip. "The shit you geek-ass screenwriters think about, and never mind the geek-ass way you verbalize it. You think I bother to keep count?" He put a finger to Jonah's stomach and swirled it in the impressive amount of precome there, then brought it to his mouth and licked it off his finger. He closed his eyes and smiled, then rolled Jonah higher up on his back and fucked into him three times quick, in and out.

Jonah groaned, loud and long, squeezing his hands tight around his thighs. He raised his head and looked in awe at Slater's dick sinking inside him. "Jesus."

"What?" Slater slowed. The mattress stopped creaking.

"Nothing." Jonah dropped his head, but Slater was still watching him. His pupils were down to pinpricks, but it wasn't anything new, and Jonah didn't bother himself about it. "So...so everything going okay down there?"

Slater raised an eyebrow at him and stopped moving. "Can't you tell?"

Jonah squinted, closed one eye shut and peered sheepishly up at Slater with the other. He shrugged. "I guess. Feels good."

"Hell yeah, it feels good." Slater looked at Jonah speculatively. "Shit. You're an ass virgin, aren't you? Man, I thought those were extinct."

Jonah tried to look scornful. "You think I'm a virgin."

Slater ignored him. "So some little chick never pegged your ass?"

Jonah put an arm over his face. "No," he muttered into his arm.

Slater pried his arm away. He studied Jonah a moment. "Oh, okay. I get it." He peered exaggeratedly at Jonah's ass and laughed when Jonah gave him an exasperated look. "You're fine, Prudence. Clean as a whistle. Good enough to eat." He winked.

Jonah flushed but tried to rally as a matter of pride. "The No Rimming sign's already posted. Be happy your dick was in before the yellow flag went up or nothing would have hit this beach."

Slater rolled his eyes and started moving again. "I'll go slow. Been a long time since I popped cherry."

"You keep up this pace and I'm going back to sleep. Where, I may add, I was perfectly happy without a dick up my ass," Jonah said.

Slater pulled nearly all the way out and then rolled his hips, sinking back in slow and easy. Again, a little faster. "Yeah? I don't think so." He pushed in hard, spine arching back, knees digging into the bed.

"Oh, fuck, that's—yeah. More. Like that." Jonah groaned, writhing.

"Like that?"

"Oh fuck, yeah." Jonah slammed his head down on the mattress, gasping. "Should I call you Devin now you're in balls deep? Slater feels unnecessarily formal, don't you think?"

Slater smiled, a feral grin that said he was pleased with himself and the world, then gave up and laughed outright, head thrown back. "You're fucking with my rhythm, man," he bitched, then looked down at Jonah, still grinning. He fucked in harder, each time sliding Jonah further up the mattress.

Jonah closed his eyes, wished like hell they'd put a new sheet on after dragging the other one off (because who the hell knew who else had been fucked on that sheet—and on this mattress, come to think of it). He felt the drag of cock inside him, opening him up, and then the bastard hit his prostate, bump, slide, and Jonah propped himself on the bed with his elbows and yelled up at the ceiling, *oh fuck* and *Jesus*.

Slater grinned again. "Sweet spot," he crooned, looked smug and did it again. Jonah gave a full-out roar this time, white sparks disintegrating before his eyes. His cock bobbed against his stomach, begging, and Slater jerked him once, twice, until Jonah went off like a rocket in the deep blue yonder.

"You are mine, motherfucker," Slater said, beaming like nothing would ever swipe that motherfucking grin off his face. Jonah winked at him tiredly and gave him a free bump and grind. "Fucking fuck," Slater groaned, hips thrusting. Jonah grabbed at the mattress, trying to keep his head from banging into the headboard.

"Shit, motherfucker, hot damn you've got an ass on you," Slater said, coming hard, back bowed and rammed in deep. Jonah nodded in agreement and laced his hands behind his head after Slater grew still. He closed his eyes.

Instead of relaxing, Slater's body grew stiff, muscles in his arms and chest bunching up in hard ridges. Jonah opened his eyes again.

Slater's gaze met his, eyes opening wide, wider, whites showing all around. He reared back and splayed a hand out over his chest, the fingertips white, digging into his skin. Slater grimaced. "Damn. Jonah, I think—" His face purpled and suddenly he was gasping, veins standing out in his throat.

"Shit, what's wrong, what is it?" Jonah said, panicked. He pushed Slater's hand aside and put a hand on his chest. Slater's heart was trip-hammering. "No no no no." He grasped Slater's face in his hands. His skin was clammy. "You're gonna be okay, listen, all right? I'll get a doctor."

Slater collapsed onto Jonah. He pushed himself up on his hands, made it up again a few inches. His arms trembled. He was still inside Jonah, softening. Jonah shrank against the bed, couldn't help it.

"Don't tell 'em I went out on blow, okay?" Slater whispered. Jonah could barely hear him. "Fuckers in the band will expect that."

"You're not dying on me, you're not, you hear me?" Jonah grabbed Slater's wrist, trying to count and get a pulse. It was slow, too slow, but his own panicked heartbeat got in the way of counting. He thought about CPR, but he'd never learned how to do it.

He gripped Slater's face again, shook him a little. Slater's eyes rolled back into his head, the whites snapped with red.

"Tell 'em I died on your dick," Slater gasped out. His body slumped over Jonah's.

"Shit, no, no, Slater, breathe, Jesus. Hey, hey, Devin," Jonah said. His fingers stroked Slater's cheeks. "Wake up," he whispered. "C'mon, c'mon back. Please? They'll never believe I fucked you to death, man. And I lied about the kissing. See?" He tipped Slater's blue mouth to his and kissed him. "Rimming too. Now get up."

Slater didn't move. His body was dead weight. Jonah was suddenly horrified by the feel of Slater's wet dick at his asshole. He pushed him away hard, and Slater rolled bonelessly to his side. His eyes were still open.

"Goddammit, not Slater! Why'd you have to do this?" Jonah shouted at the ceiling. The ceiling stayed quiet. So did the house.

Slater lay curled up on his side and stared at Jonah with his wide-open eyes.

After a while, Jonah turned his forehead to Slater's and rested it there. "Death by ass, huh? If that's what you want, I'll tell 'em. Jagger will shit green envy." Slater didn't answer. Jonah patted his hair, slid a hand around his neck and rubbed his skin to try and wake him. He waited for Slater to breathe. Slater didn't.

If you enjoyed this story, you can discuss it with other readers and the author at *The Band Plays On* story page at http://forbiddenfiction.com/library/story/TB1-1000003.

Less Than a Day

Annabeth Leong

Tod is a harbinger of imminent death. He doesn't use his powers for good—instead, he offers women a last fuck before they die. Jaded, Tod is surprised when one woman gets to him like no other. The last sex of her life is the best sex of his.

Less Than a Day

"You've got less than a day to live," he whispered in her ear. "Want to fuck?"

Unlike most pickup lines, the setup was true. At first glance, she could have been any single woman at the bar with blonde hair, strappy shoes, and overdone makeup and expectations; but she was the one whose imminent passing he felt in his bones. He, on the other hand, could not have been just any man. He was over six feet tall, thin as a rail, with a stone face and a cock just as hard. His hair and eyes were blacker than emptiness, and his heart was emptier than space.

The woman he'd approached blinked and pulled back from him. As if his physical appearance wasn't enough to tell her he was different, he'd dressed like an apparition as well. He wore a tailored black suit, a blood-red tie, a silver watch, and shoes polished bright enough to reflect the bit of moonlight that crawled through the bar window.

"Want to what?" the woman said.

"You heard me," he said out loud, settling into the bar stool beside her. "Want. To. Fuck. Question mark."

He didn't use his powers for good–not particularly. He told himself he used them at face value. The women he liked best had terminal diseases. They already felt death's cold shadow, and they were desperate and hungry for him, whatever he offered. They didn't care if his pronouncement was true per se. He did not like the women who thought they were immortal, the ones who laughed and told him to talk to some muscle-bound boyfriend, the ones who brushed him off with a flip of their hair and didn't even remember him in their final moments.

This woman was neither. She stared. "I did hear that part," she said. "I think I asked the wrong question."

"I can repeat the first sentence also, if you'd like." He leaned close and smiled. Now was the time to set her at ease. If he'd thrown her sufficiently off guard with his bald opening, she would like him for an upturning of the lips here, a soft touch to the cheek there. If she believed what he said, she would need him then.

"Okay," she said.

He moved his stool closer. He gestured to the bartender and ordered two club sodas. He waited until he had the drinks before turning back to her. "You've got less than a day to live," he said.

"You'd think you'd order me a stiffer drink," she said. "How do you know?"

He just smiled and looked down at the bubbles in his drink. The bar was dark and noisy. He knew just how his face looked in shadow, and how quiet could spread in a ring around him in even the loudest places.

"Okay," she said again.

He glanced up quickly. Her eyes were green like the dress she wore, but he thought they'd be blue when she was naked. She nodded slowly, and he let the grin spread over his face.

He held out a hand and helped her off the stool, led her out of the bar with firm and rapid steps.

"You don't look like the type who came in a car," she said, once they'd ducked out of the bar's back entrance and smelled the comparatively fresh air of the alley outside.

"I didn't."

The night was warm, but he noticed that her nipples were hard under her dress, and the faint hairs on her arms stood on end. The moon was nearly full.

"We can take mine," she said. Now she led, with the same fearlessness he'd displayed. Her car was an expensive red number, nicer than her forlorn little cocktail dress had led him to expect. She walked to the passenger side to let him in — an oddly chivalrous gesture.

"What do you do?" he asked as he settled his long body into the front seat.

She fiddled with her purse and put on lip balm. "Do you really care?"

He blinked. "I suppose not."

"Don't ask me any questions like that. If what you say is true, I don't want to waste any time talking about things that don't matter." She adjusted her mirrors and started the car. "Do you have a name?"

"Tod."

"Todd?" she said hopefully.

"Tod," he repeated.

"That's cute." Her voice was dark. "I do know a little German, you know."

He didn't feel the need to respond. He watched her drive. She frowned as she looked at the road, hunched forward a little to grip the steering wheel.

"We're going to my place, in case you care," she said.

"I figured."

"You do this a lot," she said. It wasn't a question. "What do you usually do?"

"What do you mean?"

She shot her eyes in his direction. "I don't want a quickie."

"Of course not. You should make sure to get what you want."

"Is that what you always say?"

"Most people don't ask. They just expect me to fuck them."

"I think," she said slowly, "that *I* want to fuck *you*."

She wasn't urgent about any of it. They parked outside her house and she took him in, pausing to take off her shoes and put her jacket away tidily. Her house was full but orderly, with a lot of feminine touches like couch covers with blue embroidered flowers. She made them both tea, which he accepted.

"Am I going to find out who or what you actually are?" she asked. She sat in a light wooden chair at her kitchen table, her legs crossed at the ankles.

"No."

"Do you know anything about how I'm going to die?"

"No."

"Then I think I'm done talking. My room's around the corner to

24

the left. Go take off your clothes and get in my bed. I'll be in as soon as I clean up the tea."

He almost offered to do it for her. Instead, he shook his head and did as she asked. He stroked himself slowly as he waited, idly reading the titles on her bookshelf. He felt her books must have all been gifts — they formed no cohesive picture of her.

She came in and paused in the doorway. "You look hot like that," she said. "Do people say that a lot?"

His hand stilled on his cock. "I don't think they usually care."

"I do. I wouldn't want my last fuck to be just anyone." She nodded toward his cock. "Don't let me stop you."

She stepped closer to the bed when he resumed stroking and pulled her dress up over her head. Her motions were slow and deliberate, but not lewd. Despite himself, he held his breath waiting for a glimpse of her nipples. She hadn't been wearing a bra. They popped out of the tight dress, dark and pointy, and he moaned in the back of his throat.

"You want me." She sounded surprised.

"Of course I do," he said. "Come here."

She stepped toward him before she'd gotten the dress off all the way. Her face still hidden in it, she shrieked when he pulled her down beside him and started biting those nipples. He let her struggle with the dress as he sucked and bit. He had her nipples poking out obscenely from each of her tits, her hips rolling against him.

She'd relaxed in his arms with her face still covered and her hands still tangled in the dress. He took the opportunity to find out how hard he could bite her breast. He fastened his teeth on her left nipple and slowly increased the pressure, listening to her whimper become a moan and her moan become a scream. He stopped short of drawing blood, but she never asked him for mercy — she only rubbed her cunt against his leg.

She fought free of the dress when he released her. "Are you going to laugh at me if I ask you to wear a condom?"

He produced one from where he'd stashed it under the pillow. "*I'm* not about to die," he said.

"Right. That makes sense." She took a deep breath. For a moment, he thought she would cry. Then she visibly hardened. "Put it on. I want to ride your cock."

He did as she asked. She didn't kiss him or make any romantic gestures. When he was ready, she supported herself with her right hand as she maneuvered herself into place. He helped her spread her cunt lips for him. She was dripping wet, and he wondered when she'd gotten that way. She sank down onto his cock with one smooth gesture, grinding against him at the end. "Ah, God," she said, her head thrown back. "Do you know how long it's been?"

"There's only one thing I know about you," he said. He put his hands on her hips to help her, but she didn't need his help. She was already pounding him, one hand on the wall beside the bed and the other on his chest.

He watched her ride him. He was turned on and ready for her, but the way she moved relaxed him. She was content to fuck herself with his cock. He didn't need to do anything in particular for quite some time.

He toyed with her, pinching her thighs or her nipples or her sides. She fucked him, rubbing her clit, squeezing her nipples, slipping her fingers into her mouth and then down to her clit once they were spit-covered and then back to her mouth once they were cunt-covered.

Sometimes, she slowed. For a while, she lowered herself so she rested on his chest and ground her clit against his pelvis while she squeezed his cock hard with her cunt. She sat up after that and leaned back so her breasts thrust out, bracing herself with one hand on his thigh behind her. Keeping her body still, she brought her free hand to her clit and masturbated ostentatiously. He didn't think it was for his benefit. Instead, she masturbated with his body. The idea turned him on. He felt his cock getting harder inside her.

He couldn't believe her wrist wasn't tired. She circled her fingers over her clit with ferocious intensity, sweating, gasping in frustration every time she didn't quite climax. Eventually, she came so hard he could clearly feel her spasming even through the condom.

While she was still coming, she resumed fucking him, really slamming down on him now. For the first time he groaned, his eyelids falling closed. He reached out for her. He wanted to fuck her back. He wanted to arch up into her and come. He wanted to push deep into her, and pull back only so he could push into her again.

"Don't you dare come yet, you motherfucker," she said then, her voice coming tight through clenched teeth. "Don't you fucking dare come."

He opened his eyes and stared at her. She was biting her lower lip, gripping his shoulders while she fucked him hard. Her hair hung around her face in sweaty threads, and sweat dripped down her back and off the points of her tits. Her eyes were hooded and dazed, staring vacantly into his face and seeing something far beyond.

He couldn't help himself. He grabbed her and pulled her down into a hard thrust. Once. Twice. Three times, and that was it. He groaned and came while she still tried to ride him. He heard her above him, saying, "Damn it, damn it, damn it."

Feeling her tight pussy still moving while he came drained him all the way.

She came to a crashing stop on top of him. "You couldn't wait?"

He shook his head, his cock still throbbing with the pleasure of it.

"I was so close to coming again."

"I can take care of that." He wouldn't have said it normally, but he wanted to make it up to her.

She cocked her head, relenting a little.

He eased her gently off his cock and got rid of the condom. Then he pushed her onto her back and lowered his lips to her pussy. It tasted a little unpleasant there, what with the latex and the sweat and the smell of his own body. But she grabbed his head right away and pulled him in.

"Don't think you're doing me a favor just by licking it," she hissed.

Startled again, he wrapped both arms around her ass and thighs and dove in. He nibbled at her labia, and when she moaned and pushed up against his face, he bit them. He nipped her clit, drooled all over her, fucked her with his tongue.

He shoved fingers up her cunt. He put one in her ass and sucked her clit hard.

"Christ, yes!" she shouted. "Don't stop!" He sucked as hard as he could, sure that he must be hurting her. She screamed but never loosened her hand on his head. He felt her starting to come, her whole body convulsing, jackknifing at a pace all her own.

"Fuck, fuck, fuck," she said. "Can you fuck me again?"

Eating her had gotten him hard. He fumbled for a condom as she clutched at him. When he finally had it on, he grabbed her legs and held them up so he could really spear her.

"Just do it hard," she said. "Make yourself come."

"Yes, ma'am." He plunged in and out of her, pulling all the way out every time and shoving fiercely back in. Since he'd already come once, he couldn't have gone too fast if he'd wanted to. Besides, she was almost purring under him. He looked down at her, off in her own world with his cock.

He gripped her harder and drilled her more forcefully. He let himself make his own private world, too, one where all he had to think about was her cunt.

She had her hand down between them, working her clit, and then she was coming again, growling from the back of her throat as she did. For a moment after she came, she felt really loose around him. He pumped harder, trying for the bit of stimulation he got around his head when he drove in really far.

She screamed a little when he pushed in that deep, and soon her pussy was clenching so tight around his cock that the sensation traveled up to his lungs and he felt like he couldn't breathe.

She was talking to him again, a stream of obscenities and anonymous filth. He hadn't thought she had this in her. The dirtiness of it made him speed up, trying not to touch the bed at all. She moved her hand out of the way and held herself up for him with a fist under each hip.

He gasped and came again.

He resisted sagging onto her body until she pulled him down. His arms were weak from exertion and he couldn't hold himself up against her force. Everywhere their skin touched he felt hot and sticky.

She kissed his forehead and lay still beneath him. "You lasted longer than I thought you would."

"Thanks." He felt annoyed with her. He shifted so he could roll away.

She stopped him with a hand on his shoulder. "So what happens now? How long do I have left?"

"The thing I do isn't very precise," he said.

Her breath was slow, considering what had just passed between them. He was still panting. "So now you leave. And I wait here alone."

He sighed. He did roll off now, and she didn't try to prevent him. He got rid of the second condom and looked at her. She would probably have been embarrassed by what he saw—smeared makeup, wild hair, sweat-soaked skin, bruises starting on her breasts from where he'd been biting her. But he liked it.

He lay on his back with his head pillowed on his folded arms. "I always leave before I see the death," he said. "The actual death... leaves a bad taste in my mouth."

She stared at him, incredulous. Then she burst out laughing. She tried to stop herself with a fist in her mouth, then gave up and rolled over, burying her face in the pillow as her shoulders shook with it. He waited. Again, he felt the need to make it up to her, though he couldn't have explained why.

A moment later he realized she was crying, not laughing. He lifted a hand to touch her shoulder but did not.

"I'm such an idiot," she choked out finally. "Right up to the end. Idiot."

"What? Why? You seem like so much less of an idiot than–" He trailed off, certain the comparison would not please her.

"Less of an idiot than the other dumb, desperate girls you fuck?" She sat up now, wiping the last of her mascara off with vigorous fists digging into the corners of her eyes. "High praise, coming from you." She sagged a little. "But I'm not less of an idiot. You see, I thought you were going to keep me company until the end. I thought I wouldn't have to die alone. But that's not what you were promising at all, was it? You were just offering me a last fuck. Which is exactly what you said. And I thought I was so clever and so sexy."

He clutched at her, suddenly fervent. "You were sexy. You were sexy as hell."

She shivered. "Let's not talk about heaven and hell right now."

"Fine." He sighed. He felt heavier than usual.

Her eyes mauled his face. "So what could I offer that would get

29

me a little more company? I've got some valuables here. You could take them if I really die."

"I'm not a thief."

"Of course not." She picked at her sweat-soaked bed-sheets. "Listen, if you're going to leave, you'd better get out of here."

He watched her eyes — blue now, as he'd guessed–shimmering with barely captured tears. She was right. Now was the time to leave.

But instead of getting up and looking for his clothes, he took her in his arms with a tenderness that surprised even him. He tilted her face up and kissed the corners of her eyes, flicking his tongue out to taste the salt there. He kissed her lips and her jaw and the hollow of her throat.

"What are you doing?" she whispered.

"I don't know."

He returned to her lips. She hesitated, but soon kissed back.

"Do you want to fuck me again?" she asked finally.

"I could, maybe, but I don't have to."

"Can I ask you for a favor?"

"You can ask."

"Will you sleep with me?"

He hesitated. She rolled away so he couldn't see her eyes. "Just for a few hours," she said quickly. "I'm tired, but I don't want to be alone. Then you can wake me up if you want, and — "

He put his hand over her mouth. He didn't want to hear her promises or her negotiations. Still silent, he turned her so her back was cradled against his chest, her ass against his pelvis. He draped one arm over her chest and palmed a breast. He lay there stiffly for a moment, then let his face roll forward into her hair.

"Do you swear you'll be here when I wake up?"

"You're going to have to trust me," he said. He wasn't going to swear.

Her body felt small and tight with tension. She smelled of sweat more than anything else. It wasn't a bad smell.

He counted her breaths, noticed the count getting slower. She uncoiled in his arms. He worried she might die that way and he wouldn't realize at first that he held a corpse. He wished death were as simple as this uncoiling, the relaxing that marked the crossing from waking to sleep.

He slipped into sleep beside her, so easily that he didn't know it until the dreams came.

"You don't have a wallet, or keys, or even money," she said. "What are you?"

He sighed. "Do you wake every man up by telling him you went through his clothes while he slept?"

"You were awake. I saw your breathing change."

"True." He opened his eyes. She had washed her face and put on a thin tank top that just covered her nipples and the curve of her ass.

"Were you having nightmares?"

He made his face as hard as he could.

"It woke me up," she admitted. "You were struggling in your sleep. And whimpering."

"Whimpering." He made the word drip with disapproval. He sat up in bed. His head felt heavy and foggy. For a moment, he wondered if she'd put something in the tea.

"You don't have to tell me." Her face began to close off from him. Absurdly, he had to stop that.

He reached for her, pulled her against his still naked chest. He stroked her hair and breathed the smell of her like she was something he would care to remember. "I did have a dream," he whispered finally. "A nightmare of you, of death in the pool."

She shivered in his arms. "Is that what's going to happen to me?"

He ignored her and went on. "I did other things, was with other people. But that image of you kept coming in. I started running, but everywhere I went, it was all I saw, and every voice I heard belonged to you."

She didn't speak for a long time. He thought she'd fallen asleep again, until she rolled to face him. "Thanks for staying." She kissed him slowly, her lips soft and warm against his, and just a little sticky.

His arms tightened around her. He realized how hard he held

her when her back cracked. He jumped and released her, but he felt her shake her head into the kiss. He wrapped her again, as tightly as loneliness.

"I could love you, maybe," she whispered. "If I weren't about to die. I think you need that."

"Don't," he said.

"Sshh," she said. "Right now, I want to pretend." She rolled onto her back, pulling his weight onto her. "What if I loved you so much that you could do anything you wanted with me? What if every touch felt good, no matter what?"

"What are you talking about?" He stiffened with alarm. She made him feel young, inexperienced, uncertain. Ridiculous.

"Bite me," she breathed. "Right at the base of my neck. As hard as you can."

In her dark bedroom, her blue eyes looked black as his. Slowly, he lowered his teeth to her neck and bit hard. She gasped in pain, fisted her hands. "Make me bleed," she said.

It was harder than he would have thought. He bit and sucked and pulled, trying and failing for a long time to tear the skin of her neck. People seemed so fragile, always ready to die, and yet a body resisted damage so steadfastly. She sobbed and struggled, but every time he almost let up, she begged for more. Finally, a trickle of iron flavor at his lips alerted him to a little wound in her neck. She sucked air between her teeth. "It stings. Bite my tits."

He bit her nipple harder than he ever had with anyone. He took it firmly between his teeth and pulled back until she cried out and honestly fought him. He grabbed her hands to hold her down and pulled some more. He tore at her nipple until she called him every filthy name and her body arched against his, her thighs wrapped tightly around him and her slick cunt frantically rubbing against his leg. The nipple bled more than her throat had. When he switched to the other, she screamed that she would kill him. He ignored her and mauled it, chewing and tugging and feeling a type of lust he never had before.

By the time he released her and looked down at her two wounded breasts, she'd become passive. When he spread her legs and bit her clit, she didn't move to stop him—just turned her head and sobbed into the pillow. He fastened his teeth around that most sensitive spot and tightened his jaw slowly, until he'd sunk deep into her flesh. Her sobs turned high-pitched. He shoved three fingers up her cunt and felt it squeezing down around them.

"I love you," she breathed. "I love you. I love you." And came.

He couldn't stand it. He opened his mouth and let go of her, pulled his fingers out, and flipped her over so he didn't have to look at her face. He spread the cheeks of her ass.

"Please," she said. He wet his fingers and pushed them slowly into her asshole, relishing each jerk her body gave as they penetrated her. A tear fell onto the blanket, but she shifted feebly, opening herself to him a little more. He added another finger and another, listening to the way her breathing changed as he further filled her.

He eased his hand out of her ass and found another condom. He spat on it, and on her asshole as well, and worked himself into her. He could feel the pulse moving through her skin. His body rose and fell each time her lungs expanded and released. He kissed the nape of her neck and bore down with his cock until he'd made it all the way in.

She sighed and lifted her ass up to him. He dug his fingers into her shoulders and levered himself into her, harder and harder. Suddenly, he wanted to hurt her, to enjoy every desperate sound she made. He gave her everything he had. He pounded her until his muscles screamed. He nailed her to the bed beneath him. She'd stopped speaking words, moaning inarticulately as she found her clit with her fingers again.

She had nowhere to go. He had her completely. As his cock spurted, he whispered into her hair, making sure she couldn't hear, "You too."

The feeling that rose in his chest frightened him. He pulled his cock out and stood. He had to get away. "Don't leave," she whispered. "Stay with me until the end."

He didn't say a word, just found his clothes and pulled them on. He already felt the mess on his cock soiling his clothes and soaking through his underwear. Right then, he didn't care.

She lay still on the bed, face buried in her arms. Before he walked out of the room, he grabbed a fistful of her hair and lifted her head. Her eyes seared him, full of fire and betrayal, reflecting memories of his own that he couldn't stand to think about. He almost asked her name, but thought better of it. She didn't try to stop him again.

He would normally have left a long time before, maybe even whistling to himself as he walked down a black and silent street, smelling of sour sweat and feeling alive. He let himself out, crossed the street, but could go no further. The night looked different to him. Part of him had stayed inside his dream, and he imagined he heard her voice. For the first time in a long time, he wanted a cigarette. And a drink.

Would her house catch fire? Would she die of some medical condition, leaving no sign of when it had happened? Would a masked man come to her door and find his way inside?

He stood in the shadows across from her door and watched. It was not yet dawn. He had to go, before he learned answers he didn't want to know to questions he didn't want to have. She had threatened to love him. He shivered.

Several blocks away, a shadow lengthened under the streetlights and drifted closer. Death would be here soon. He could go back to her, hold her hand as she stared into those grave-hollow eyes—but he would have to see them, too. He watched the shadow grow, measuring his own courage and finding it wanting.

The first fingers of light grasped the bottom of the sky. He spat on the sidewalk and turned away.

If you enjoyed this story, you can discuss it with other readers and the author at the *Less Than a Day* story page at
http://forbiddenfiction.com/library/story/AL1-1.000030.

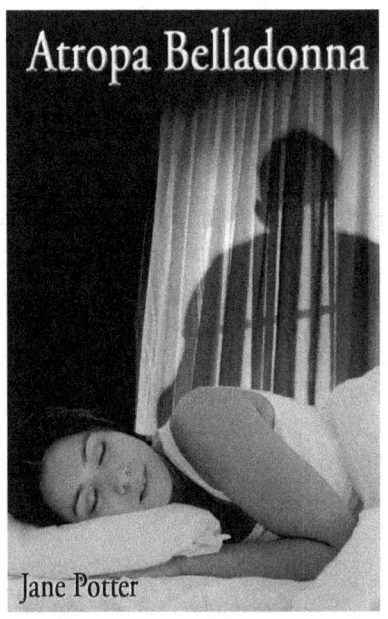

Atropa Belladonna

Jane Potter

When something tall, fanged and handsome crawls out of the darkness to confess his love and devotion, she finds it hard to resist. But when sexual ecstasy turns to nightmarish possession, it becomes apparent that it's equally hard to run away.

Chapter 1
Little Deaths

One of his hands is on your ankle, cold and clamped like a leech, and the other one is sliding slowly up the inside of your thigh. Tension ratchets higher and higher inside of you as it moves up, but it's tauntingly slow and it doesn't even graze the wetness of your cunt, just curves around the slope of your ass and squeezes it like a ripe fruit. You can't see, but you can feel him grinning.

Face down on the mattress, you let out a harsh groan, muffled in the sheets. Hitching your hips up to beg mutely doesn't work. Your cunt throbs, exposed and untouched.

"Shh," he murmurs, his voice papery and thin. Something in it scrabbles like rat's claws against your skin. Something beneath his vocal cords and his clever tongue and his fine, sculpted mouth, flushed red with blood and sex.

Shivering, you go still again. You remember that he likes it when you don't move. Stay still.

Play dead.

A hysterical giggle tries to bubble up from your chest.

His mouth is suddenly right beside your ear, stubble scraping your cheek. "You're so beautiful when you sleep," he whispers. "I could look at you forever."

There is ice in his skin and carrion on his breath.

In the morning, the window is still open.

The thing is —

The thing is you're an adult, but this whole thing is like something out of a children's story, horror that suddenly seems far too awful to inflict on a child now that you know first-hand what it's like when the story is real. You can't believe people think things like this are fun, consume them as entertainment and laugh off the idea that they might actually be horrible.

You did that. Once.

You can't just pack up and leave, is the thing; you've got a life here and you can't just abandon it. Every day you go and have your life that exists in the sunlight (carworklunchbills) and every day you find yourself at the dry cleaners or the gas station or the grocery store (moneyhousefood) and suddenly it hits you how impossible it is. How could this life possibly exist in the same reality as the life where you know cold flesh and terrifying dark eyes and the subtle scent of rot in clammy sheets?

That daylight life is what lets you get into bed every night. Makes you think this time it's not going to happen, he won't be there—he can't be there. Things like him don't happen.

But you realise that you know better once it's dark outside. Every fibre of your body knows; every instinct and every ounce of self-preservation in your blood screams with terror.

Sleep is a horror, a wordless looming nightmare. The very thought of it makes you want to retch. You catch a glimpse of yourself in the mirror and you look like a wreck. You drink coffee and taurine and take pills until your hands shake, vision blurring, headache throbbing like an ice pick through your sinuses, bones grinding down as if the span of two days without sleep is a physical weight.

Barely conscious and still half dazed from the medication, you drag the comforter off your mattress and crawl underneath the bed, where some buried part of you murmurs that it's safe and dark and hidden, safe, safe. Never find you here.

Hours later, you wake up with a jolt, heart beating frantically against the insides of your ribcage, ohgod ohgod ohgod, what is it? What happened? You don't know, you don't know.

A floorboard creaks.

You lay there in the dark for what feels like hours, body rigid against the floor with terror like a vice grip around your joints. Dust makes your nose prickle and tears sting at your eyes. Don't cry. You can't cry, you can't, he'll hear—but a tear wells out of one eye and slides down your cheek, a silent leaking trail that bumps over the corner of your mouth and hits the floor with an audible plick.

You hold your breath and pray with every fibre of your body that you're alone.

A sudden moan thrums through the house, enough to make your whole body jump so hard that your muscles hurt. Your stomach is still twisting and rolling as you realise that it's just the furnace coming on, old machinery in the basement groaning to life.

Trembling all over, you press your cheek against the floor and try to breathe as the house sighs and settles around you, faint ticks and cracklings running through the walls, letting off frissons of tension accumulated during the day. The air underneath the bed is as musty as a grave.

The creak in the corner of the room is sudden and close.

Nothing. It's nothing—

Until there's another one, and then a third, slow and deliberate coming across the room, and they're footsteps, one after the other.

Out of the corner of your eye, you see him lay down a patent leather shoe with utmost care, heel ball toe as gently as a cat, slow and menacing. He's not trying to be quiet. If he was, you'd never hear him. He's playacting his presence, giving you a chance to assume your role now: the sweet girl, glad to see him, short of breath and squirming with arousal, thighs pressed tight together against the throb of pleasure but absolutely ready to spread them in an instant when he wants you to.

You don't.

He stands there. He knows.

"Sweetheart," he says, cool amusement in his voice, and you jump even though you're expecting it. You jam a knuckle in your mouth to stifle the tears that threaten to overwhelm you. "What are you doing under there?"

You're thinking, playing it out in your head like that's going to change anything. Feverish ideas unspool rapidly, your brain working fast and sharp in this place where you're beyond panic, beyond fear. You realise that it was a bad idea to wrap yourself up in the comforter;

it's tucked around your legs and you won't be able to kick. So he'll grab your ankles and drag you out, and you're going to have to grab the slats of the bedframe overhead — not the horizontal slats but the wooden crossbeam that runs head to toe across them, the crux where the two overlap so that you can hook your fingers around something and not lose grip. They're going to dig into your fingers, edges of the wood hard against soft thin flesh right down to the bone, cutting deep, but you'll hold on, you have to, there's no choice about it and people can do extraordinary things when they have to —

But he says nothing, does nothing else. After a while there's a faint chuckle, the kind of sound adults make when children are being ridiculous, and his polished leather shoe moves out of your line of sight.

Too scared to break the stillness, you lay there trembling in the dust until you can hear birds singing and there's a thick stripe of full, gold sunlight on the floorboards beyond the shade of the bed, the sounds of cars and garage doors opening and some ambitious neighbour's lawn mower starting up on the street outside, and it's morning.

He comes back.

You knew he would.

You knew and you did nothing, all because — because it was easier to play stupid, to lie to yourself. Because you couldn't deal with this if it was really real, there and happening and happening to you. (Because things like this don't happen to good girls.) So what right do you have to feel like dying the next time you hear the soft scrape of the window sliding up in its casing? You were the one who decided to stay.

It's thirty degrees out and you've been sweating like a pig in the sweltering Canadian prairie summer, leaving damp patches on a pillowcase that doesn't have a cool side left. Your pajamas cling to sweat-sticky skin, rucked up in awkward spots; heat lies like a heavy blanket in the tucks of your body, your pits and your crotch and the backs of your knees where cotton pants can't bunch up any higher. You can feel heat pouring off of you in waves.

You can feel (you imagine you can feel) the chilled spot where your heat bounces back off the cold body behind you like echolocation, reflecting a shiver that crawls down your back with spidery claws.

His arm slips over the bend of your waist, touching skin where your t-shirt rides up high on your ribs, twisted halfway around your body, and you don't move, you don't fucking move, every muscle clamped so hard you could break with a breath.

Goosebumps rise and ripple along your arms when his fingers touch your belly, fingers cold as the underside of a stone. They slide down, raising invisible hairs the whole way, and your body clutches and your hands grip and your heart races until it hurts.

You are so fucking wet that you can feel it between your thighs.

What started it first? You don't know, whether it was the muggy summer heat that made your sleep turn sweaty or the dream that happened to mimic the weather, or the fact that fucking is literally all you've been able to think about for days. It just was, just indistinct impressions of bodies and sex that left your panties wet and your cunt heavy with unfulfilled need. But now you want to clamp your thighs shut, rub them hard together, shove your fingers inside and ride your hand until you burst—you want all that.

That's the worst thing. He's going to give it to you and you want it.

His hand pushes underneath the waistband of your pants, the elastic of your panties. Then his fingers are on your cunt, as cold as if he's been standing in the rain for an hour (there hasn't been any rain), and oh, God—

"Oh God," you slur, the side of your face pressed into the pillow. He laughs.

Your legs, you just fucking hitched them open, jolt-reaction without thinking for a second. So what right do you have to complain, now?

The sensation of it is amazing, his long fingers delving through your damp-hot curls to curl around your pubic bone and slide down against the slick heat of your cunt. The sharp contrast makes you shudder, body accidentally pressing back into the curve of his. Humiliation grabs you by the throat, but that doesn't change the fact that you can feel the folds of your cunt pulsing with blood around his chilly, stroking fingers.

"You're so beautiful," he whispers behind your ear, his nose buried deep in your hair like he's breathing the heat, the scent of your skin and sweat and salt. "Perfect. Just fucking perfect."

His breath is hot, and you shiver and you want to believe. He strokes his fingers up and down the length of your slit, slow and sensuous and deliberate. Pleasure thrums through your whole body, wound up tight as a harpstring ready to sing, scream. He knows how to play you.

Your voice is thin, croaky, doesn't quite work. "Please—"

"Shh," he murmurs, his other hand coming up to lay a finger against your lips and press them shut. He shifts behind you, craning over your shoulder so that he can nuzzle the wet-sheened hollow of your clavicle and the side of your throat.

His fingers trail ice against the sweltering throb of your cunt, confident and talented. Little noises break in your throat as he fingers you slowly, thumb circling the swollen nub of your clit. You shake with the intensity of it, pleasure cracking through your limbs like heat lightning. It's bright and constant and too much, too much contact with your hypersensitive flesh.

You try to shift away and his arm clamps down like a steel band, pinning your hips in place against his.

Desperate, you sob, "Jesus," jerking your hips as hard as possible in an effort to get his thumb off your clit. He pushes down harder, circling it without mercy.

He makes a stifled noise, a groan of need. Suddenly he pulls away from behind you and pulls back on your shoulder, rolling you onto your back and throwing one jean-clad knee over your legs. Straddling your thighs, he sits up tall and looms over you, dark eyes magnetic. Before you can do more than grunt, he takes the waistbands of your pants and panties and stretches them down, making space for his other hand to twist and push lower.

Two fingers push into your cunt without preamble, middle and ring fingers all the way to the third knuckle, with the titanium band on his ring finger searing cold against your labia. Your whole body seizes up, every muscle pulling tight enough to force a scream from your chest, something like God and fuck and YES.

His thumb is still working hard over your clit, wrist flicking skillfully to drive his fingers hard into your body over and over again, but you're already falling apart. You're about to come and you know it, can't believe how fast it's tearing through you, strong enough to make your eyes roll back in your head.

"Oh god, fuck, please," you say, "f-fuck—"

The walls of your cunt clamp hard around his fingers, rhythmic spasming contractions that grow harder and harder as it builds so fast that you can't breathe. All you can do is twitch and jerk and stare up at him from beneath the spear of his eyes, not knowing whether you want to scream yes or NO.

Fuck—fuck, almost, just—fingers fucking hard in and out, determined to rip out the hardest orgasm your body can have, but what does it is the fact that they're still cold in the sweltering heat of your cunt, unnatural and shocking and spreading you wide open.

Hands fisted in the sheets, you come so hard that you sit halfway up, mouth stretched open in a scream that you don't have oxygen for. There's a second of white airlessness and then it breaks over you, big throbbing pulses of pleasure as your cunt flutters and clenches hard around his fingers. His thumb on your clit is a sharp white pain, an ecstasy so intense that it hurts, but you can't, you can't get the words out, nothing but an incoherent string of, "Fuck, God, I, fuck fucking—" as you ride it out, shuddering and twitching against the mattress.

When you open your eyes again, he's sucking on his fingers, smiling down at you but visibly shaken, the bulge of his cock pressing hard against the seam of his jeans. There's a wildness in his eyes, need and fraying self-restraint. In that moment, you can't remember why you didn't want this.

He moves like a great cat, lunging down on top of you to kiss and suck his way up your throat, his movements hungry and passionate. His tongue leaves a slick trail across your clavicle, up your throat—back down to the breast he's cupping in one hand to suck on your nipple. The tightening of your nipple into a hard bud makes you choke back a moan, your whole body still flushed with the last pulses of orgasm. He rolls your nipple skillfully with his tongue, hitting it with sudden hard flicks of the tongue, then sets it between his teeth and tugs without warning. An unexpected wash of pleasure follows the initial jolt of pain.

Oh God. You can't. Not again. You—

No, it's okay, it's going to be okay, you promise yourself. Your rabbit-heart is still beating frantically, cold fear chasing down your spine. As if to fight it, you put a hand on the back of his neck and push his face harder against your breast (to which he growls in satisfaction). You can do this. You can—

You can consent to this. You want this. If you consent, then it isn't—then he's not—then there's nothing wrong with this and everything will be okay. You want this.

Your cunt is still fluttering with aftershocks and you want this.

"Yeah," you whisper, your voice crackling and parched. "I—please"

A groan gets dragged out of his chest as he pulls himself away from your tit as though it physically hurts him to do so. "You're so beautiful," he tells you fervently, nuzzling into your throat.

His tongue darts out to lick your neck. Instinct makes you wrench away immediately—but you want this, you want him, so you turn your face back, meeting the blown hazel-gold of his eyes. Your nails scrape at the back of his neck as you pull him down for a kiss instead.

A spark of pain shoots through your lip as something razor sharp grazes it. You whimper and let his tongue chase its way into your mouth.

One of your shaking hands moves down to cup the heavy bulge in his jeans. The noise he makes into your mouth is gratifying, terrifying. A button, a zipper—a shimmy of his hips against yours to drag his jeans down just enough for his cock to spring free, precum glistening on the head.

He pushes his cock into you slowly, sinking inch by inch into your slippery cunt. The sensation makes your breath stutter in your throat, choked guttural noises at the thick, cold length pushing inexorably into your cunt, still ripe and oversensitive. His breath shaking against your neck, he withdraws and thrusts back in harder, rocking his hips into yours. The noise it makes is obscene.

"Fuck. Yes," you hiss, trying to adjust to it. (You want this.) Without meaning to, you dig your nails into his back, where muscles flex and slide powerfully beneath the skin, strength like stone and steel.

The sweat beading on his back makes his skin clammy. It smells faintly of grave earth and decay.

No. No. Oh God, think about something else. Just—

Your orgasm has faded, leaving nothing but a buzz in your blood and a warm throb in your core. Rocking your hips up against his in an attempt to urge him on faster, rougher (anything, just more distraction), you can feel a residual tightness there, tension still present in the deep soft places of your body. A kernel of heat is already building again.

Breathless, you mutter, "Make me come again."

He laughs, fucking into you harder. You hiss and shove back against him, locking your legs around his waist, yes you want this, you're in control.

But his hips, his hands—one hand settles on the wing of your pelvic arch and holds you down, easy as pinning a butterfly, and he fucks you at his own pace, thrusts languid and long, leaving you stretching and straining futilely for more.

"Oh, come on."

His lips are wet on your neck, sucking bruises into your skin. "Shh. I'll take care of you."

No. Not good enough. Not—

"I want—"

"I know what you want." He captures your mouth with his, swallowing your protest. When his teeth nick your tongue and sudden coppery heat salts the kiss, his hips jolt and then thrust into you that much faster, but it's still not enough.

His kiss feels like drowning, deep and endless and airless forever. The taste of it makes you gag, recoiling as your stomach tries to heave so hard that you choke. He mutters something indistinct and leans down to mouth at your throat instead, sharp stinging trails of pain here and there where his teeth catch. You shudder and struggle to keep your gorge down, mouth still curdled with the taste of old blood and rotten flesh.

Don't—God, don't think about it, think about something else.

You blink frantically, your mouth working as you struggle for control. Think about the way he's moving on top of you, lean muscle and effortless strength, his cock thick enough to stretch you just a little bit every time he thrusts.

Heat pulses in your cunt but he won't feed it, isn't fucking you hard enough to give you the friction you need. You try to roll your hips against him and he pins you down again, laughing.

"This isn't—"

He kisses you.

"—funny. I want—"

"I know what you want."

A whine creeps into your voice as an edge of desperation starts to coil in your core, as stalled pleasure drags on without resolution, without release. "Then fuck, Jesus Christ, just—"

It's building up, just not properly; there's no spark or crackle through your nerves, no flutter in the muscles of your cunt. Even when you try to shove him off, squirming with mingled dissatisfaction and desperation, he keeps fucking you at that same steady pace, his balls slapping against you.

You come without warning, a single clench and release of your body and then it's over, a rapidly slowing pulse, almost purely without pleasure. You rock your hips desperately, trying to grind out some spark of ecstasy from the release, but no—it's like you struck orgasm a moment too late or too early, missed it. All you get is exhaustion, oversensitivity that makes every thrust of his cock suddenly too much to bear.

You almost shriek in frustration with the spoiled orgasm, because you still want to come but you can't, your body worn out prematurely, and it feels like it could drive you mad. And you can't make him stop.

"Fuck," you spit, on the edge of tears, "you asshole—"

He suddenly pulls out, hazel eyes molten with an unexpected flash of darkness. One hand under your back, he flips you over like it's nothing, wrenches your hips up off the bed and slams back into you so hard that the whole bedframe bangs against the wall.

Your cry of shock and pain gets lost in the furious rattle of bedstead against the wall, in time with his cock pounding savagely into you. You can't breathe, can't think—all the air crushed out of your lungs, the bones of your spine rattling brutally together, teeth clicking painfully. He's fucking you like he wants to rip you to pieces, sharp savage thrusts, his cock slamming balls-deep each time. The stretch of his fingers was nothing compared to this, this, splitting you wide open and tearing you apart, clatter snap crack of bones and skin and anemic flesh—

The next time you come, it's with a scream into the mattress and the stretching burn of two cold fingers wedged deep into your spasming cunt alongside his cock, forcing you open wider than you've ever been, until you finally get your breath back enough to whimper for him to stop, yes, please, God, thank you, please.

You're asleep when it happens, slumbering uneasily through the dull aches that grip your groin until suddenly you are awake, yelping, shoved roughly onto your back. Someone rips the blankets out of your grasp and it's dark, too dark to see, but you catch a glimpse of hazel iris and dark hair limned with white in the moonlight that shafts into the room through the open window.

Trembling with shock, you freeze. "What—"

He grabs your wrist and yanks it so hard that you cry out. There's a clattering of chain, silver flashing in the moonlight, and hard metal ratchets tight around your wrist. The other end of the manacles hangs wide open.

"Oh Jesus Christ," you whisper, unable to raise your voice above a croak as sick horror rolls your stomach over. "No, I—"

You try to scrabble backwards on the bed. His knee shoves between yours, forcing them apart, and you let out a wretched moan.

Oh God, you think. You know you're going to die, it can't be anything else with the way he's climbing on top of you, his eyes wild and feverish even though his skin is colder and clammier than you've ever felt before. The scent of decay on his sweat-damp body makes you gag, sweat like putrescence leaking from a corpse.

Your arm flops limply in his grasp, too nerveless to do anything with. Straddling your waist, he leans over and pins both of your hands up against the headboard. His face is inches from yours, mouth carved in a hard, flat line, his eyelids looking thin and purple-blue from exhaustion. In the moonlight, his skin is so blanched that he looks almost lipless.

The manacles rattle against the bedframe, knocking about in the gap between the frame and the wall. What is — what —

And then the cuff around your one wrist jerks tight, drawing a sharp cry of pain from you. Pulling down — and you realise then that he's looped the cuffs around one of the slats supporting the mattress and brought the open end of the cuffs back up to snap shut around your other wrist. The sharp metal digs into bone, dragging a stifled sound of distress from your throat.

Without even looking at you, he tears at the waistband of your pajama pants, dragging them roughly down and off. You can't even protest as your underwear goes with them, even though you're on your period and you'll bleed everywhere without —

Oh. God.

Blood. You're bleeding out, slow and sticky and hot, the coarse curls around your cunt clotted with it. Even you can smell the hot copper tang in the air now that you're not wearing a pad, cunt exposed to the air.

He drags your hips to the edge of the bed unceremoniously, breathing so harshly that it's almost a snarl. Pain splinters up your arms at the jerk of your wrists against the manacles. His knees hit the floor with a loud thud. Cold fingers dig into your knees, push them open and slide up your thighs like spiders, bloated and pale from too long in the dark. And even with your heart in your throat, panic clawing hysterically at your insides, you can tell that there's something wrong with his flesh — too pallid, too drained. It's pulled papery and tight at the joints, over the sharp cheekbones of his handsome face, but as soft and sunken as an overripe fruit in other places.

His tongue shoves into your cunt without finesse, without anything but blind desperate hunger, and he moans like a dying animal.

Sparks of pain shoot out where his fingers are digging into your skin, into the yellow-green bruises still fading from your hipbones. You have to clench your hands into fists around the tight manacle chains in order to stop yourself from crying out in pain.

Trembling so hard that the handcuff chain rattles, you lie frozen, breathing as shallowly as possible. You stare at the ceiling and you listen to the grunting and the slick sucking noise of his talentless tongue, feeding without a hint of care for your pleasure.

It's as if you're listening to one half of a porno, with him groaning and sighing in gratification as he licks your labia clean before plunging his tongue back into you. A sharper moan of renewed ecstasy rips from his throat. Gluttonous, he buries his face between your legs, shoving and sucking with obscene relish.

You don't want this.

Chapter 2
To Die, To Sleep

Daytime feels like a dream, full of fragilities and blurring light and ghosts that move through the house around you without actually touching your world.

You look around your kitchen and don't recognise anything. Empty fridge, dirty stove, dirty dishes in the sink—what is all this? Whose life is this? Someone ate here (but the thought of food makes your stomach pitch and yaw dangerously, and you realise you can't remember the last time you ate). Someone wrote TV times on the calendar; someone bought buttercup-yellow hand towels and stitched a needlepoint of crocuses to hang over the microwave.

The only thing that strikes you as real is the bottle of prescription uppers sitting on the windowsill, the ones you were taking to keep awake—how long ago? Two weeks? Only that?

You pick it up, pop the cap and pour the contents out onto your hand. It's not until you feel crushing disappointment when you see that there are only two left, though, that you realise how badly you were hoping that there would be more. Enough to overdose on.

A choked laugh takes you by surprise, loud in the silence of the house. Putting yourself to sleep with a handful of stimulants—funny.

You look at the steak knives in the cutting block for just a heartbeat before you have to wrench your eyes away, stomach lurching horribly. No blood. God, no blood; you can't. Not like that.

You throw the bottle out in the garbage can just outside the back door. In a daze, you look around the back yard and wonder when your garden got so green. The lawn is long and full of clover; your flowerbeds are spilling over their bounds. The nightshade you planted around the door is almost as tall as you, its branches waving their pale purple flowers and shiny black berries over the lid of the trash can.

It's a long stretch of heartbeats before you realise that you're thinking about it, seriously considering it: how much would it take to kill you, how many of these dark little fruits you'd have to eat, if they'd be as sweet as they're said to be, how long it would take. You know damn well that this thing's poison; that's why you planted it. You liked the idea of keeping 'beautiful death' in your garden.

And then you know.

You're done. It's over. It has to be over, now, because if every little thing you look at seems to you like a way out, then this can't go on any longer.

As if on autopilot, you walk to the linen closet, pull a folded duffle bag from the top shelf.

Shirts, jeans, sweaters from the pile of unfolded laundry in the living room. Toothbrush, soap. Shampoo. You know what you're doing, but you don't think about it. You don't even let the idea occur to you, just float in this still, quiet place inside your head, where nothing touches you. It's almost as if someone else is moving your hands, folding panties with utter calm and tucking them neatly in the bag. Then socks, bras, comb, brush and tweezers. The makeup kit you haven't touched in weeks.

You collect every spare key in the house and put them in your pocket. One by one, you yank out the wires from the telephone jacks. Your cellphone gets left behind.

It's ten o'clock in the morning when you start your car and roll out of the driveway. End of the block. Turn the corner.

In your daze, some part of you is counting every turn, every block, as if half expecting to be stopped at any moment, but the neighbourhood is deserted, everyone at work.

Edge of the neighbourhood, turn left, turn left, turn right. Stoplight — red.

Green.

Busy street. Turn right. Stoplight. Stoplight.

Turn right. Go — wait — merge.

Highway.

You drive for nineteen hours, stopping only for gas and leaving burned rubber on the pavement at the pumps. Two provinces go by in a blur of farm fields and prairie towns, and the landscape starts to buckle up into mountainous foothills just past sunset. The cashier at the midnight Petro-Can, just past the British Columbia border, opens his mouth to say something, then looks at you a second time and shuts it.

You don't know how you get across the Rockies alive, without driving through the guard rail and off a cliff on some twisty mountain highway, without hitting a sheep that your headlights weren't bright enough to catch. You're frayed too thin to even be afraid. Anything in front of you can't be as bad as what's behind you. You just go through, through and out the other side. That's what your life is, now.

Right before dawn the next morning, your car limps into a motel parking lot on the other side of the Rockies, thirty-two grungy rooms and no credit card machine, cash only.

You don't remember taking off your shoes before falling into oblivion, bones weighted down with concrete and the memory of cold flesh rutting slick between your thighs.

It's dark in the motel room, nothing but stripes of orange sodium-glow slanting across the ceiling and far wall. Sleep is stale and tacky on your tongue. Groggy, you reach out and fumble for the wristwatch you left on the bedside table. Pain lances through your shoulder — stiffness that tells you how dead still you've been lying.

Okay, you think, you've slept through the day; what time is it, nine, ten o'clock? You need to get going now that the sun's down —

But it's not ten o'clock, and you see the time on the watch heart-beats after you realise how oily your skin is, how your clothes stick to your skin, how all your muscles feel like they haven't moved in months. That's what huge, long bouts of sleep feel like, longer than eight hours.

It's five-twenty and you've been sitting in one place for almost twenty-four hours and he's had all night to catch up.

A jolt of sheer, unadulterated terror burns the grogginess right out of your head. Next thing you know, you're outside in the grey pre-dawn halflight, one shoe not even totally on your foot, shivering hard at the cold morning air in nothing but a t-shirt. There's so much adrenaline burning through your bloodstream that you don't even know how you got there, can't remember the intervening seconds.

The keys clatter noisily against the metal of the car door as you scrabble for the right one. Ten seconds and you'll be spraying gravel; five seconds—

Wrest the door open, scramble in. Jam the key in the starter. Turn it—turn—

Nothing happens. No rumble, no grind of the starter—you can't even process that for a good fifteen seconds and so you keep turning the key, shoving it around so hard that your thumb is white and bloodless against the metal. There is no ignition.

Heart in your throat, you get out of the car. Gravel crunches loudly in the silent parking lot. All the motel rooms are dark, and the street lamp overhead has turned off for some reason.

In the ruddy gleam of the high-up MOTEL neon, you feel your way around to the hood of the car and pry at the latch with shaking fingers. It takes several tries for your muscles to pull hard enough to pop it open. All this time, nausea trembles in the pit of your stomach, sharp and clenching.

Oh, you think, before it really hits you, the engine's gone.

The engine's been ripped out of your car.

It takes an eternity of seconds for the obvious conclusion to strike.

A hand clamps around your upper arm, hard as steel. You scream but it's muffled in the palm of the other hand already across your mouth, nails biting into your cheek. Pain shoots up your leg as you kick out and slam your knee against the grille of the car.

Still screaming incoherently, you try to kick again, heels smashing down on anything you can get at, but an unnaturally powerful arm goes around your torso, binding your arms tight down against your chest. There's a snarl next to your ear and he lifts you up so that your feet can't connect with anything, kicking uselessly in the air. It hurts, being lifted by an arm just below your ribcage, the pressure cutting deep into the soft flesh of your stomach, and you can't breathe, can't drag a gasp of air into your lungs.

Growling, he carries you back into your motel room, throws you bodily onto the bed with an utter lack of effort.

Your head snaps back painfully on the bouncing mattress, sending white shocks of pain through your vision. Light-headed from lack of air, you reach clumsily for the bedside table, trying to drag yourself upright. Stand up, just stand up—

"Did you think you could leave me?" he demands, shoving you back down on the bed with a hand around your throat. His whole handsome face is hurt and furious, an animal gone savage from the depth of the torment it's been put through. "You're mine. You'll always be mine. I love you."

His fingers clamp around your airway like steel pincers, black with engine grease. Beneath the weight of his body, you squirm and scrape for freedom, for air, for just enough space to beg—please, I didn't mean it, don't hurt me, I'm yours. You hold his eyes with your own desperate stare, trying frantically to appeal through the ruthless fury in his expression. Tears film your eyes.

He lets go for long enough to let you get a breath. The air hits your lungs like a hammer and you scream.

His face contorts with rage and he shoves his palm down hard over your mouth again. The force of his grip mashes your lips against your teeth, and the cartilage of your nose grinds between his pinched thumb and forefinger. It takes several long seconds of twisting at this new agony before you realise that worse than that, you can't breathe. He is not going to let you breathe ever again.

A stitch of red pain tears at your chest, growing sharper with every passing moment. It's as if someone's wedging a knife into the bone of your ribs and cracking them apart. You can't see anymore, eyes glossed over with tears, can't breathe, can't move—not with his body weighing down on you, heavy as clay, eyes burning in his bloodless face. Your legs kick uselessly against the mattress, hitting his calves, but no more, nothing. And your hands, you don't know when it happened but they're pinned above your head, wrists grinding together in his fist.

He lets go with his thumb and forefinger. Pain sears through your nose as you suck frantically for air, drawing in as much as you can through bruised nasal passages.

Soft as death, he whispers, "Stay. Still."

You do. God help you but you do. Even as he takes his hand off your mouth and rips one-handed at the button of your jeans. Even as he yanks your fly open and shoves his hand into your panties.

Strung tight and trembling, you shake with the effort of silence as he strokes your clit until you're wet and dipping, humiliation sitting sick and hot in your chest. The patient and deliberate slide of his fingers is a searing counterpoint to the hand still clamped tight around your wrists, holding you down.

He narrows his eyes as he slides three fingers into you with agonising slowness, determined to see it through despite the way his wrist is twisted with the awkwardness of the angle. Hunger burns in his eyes, a low slow flame that devours everything in its path. Inexorable and ancient, with all the patience in the world, he takes you apart one piece at a time, destroying you with fingers that thrust and grind against your clit until you finally break, sobbing and coming all over his hand.

He makes you come a second time, not even pausing in between, just continuing to finger you slow and deep right through the hypersensitivity and the pain and out the other side where pain turns into pleasure again. Eyes rolling up in your head, you come with your cunt clenching around his cold fingers, juices leaking down his wrist with its blue veins full of anaerobic blood.

Boneless, you lie there with your eyes shut as he peels down your jeans, takes off your shoes and socks, and then reaches back up to pull off your sodden panties.

The third time, you're not even sure if you're screaming in ecstasy or agony. Somewhere a wire is crossed inside your head, turning everything into raw sensation that crackles through your limbs like lightning, making your toes curl and your spine arch and your fingers jerk spastically. He's silent through the whole thing, but when he presses his hand over your mouth to muffle your wails, it's a warm touch, full of affection that you can feel just from the gentle curve of his palm, a guide to soothe and help you through the aftershocks that wrack your limbs.

"You're perfect like this," you hear him say, over the roar of blood pounding in your ears. You're wrecked, quivering, broken down so far that you can't even speak. Every breath comes shaking.

He's nuzzling into your hair, the curve of your throat. Grave-stale breath makes your skin ripple with goosebumps so quickly that it's painful. "I love you so much." A long inhalation, nose pressed to the sweat-slick place between your breasts, scenting you, salt and skin. "I'd do anything for you, you know that. You're mine and I love you."

There are water stains on the ceiling. There is a tongue on your throat. There is quiet.

He sits up. Then, in a tone of delighted surprise: "Oh. Would you look at that."

You turn your head to the side slowly, exactly like a puppet with someone else's hands pushing the bones of your spine. What you see –

You don't feel anything. You see and you're empty and you don't feel anything because you just can't, because if you have to feel then it's going to be huge and choking and nauseating enough to make you puke up your insides and tear your hair out and you're going to need to die.

Dawn is in the sky outside the window, distant trees a spindly, pitch black cut-out against the wash of grey-lavender and the thin line of yellow right at the very horizon.

He slides three fingers into your cunt, which is sloppy and loose and too exhausted to do anything but quiver around his fingers as they push in deep.

"Looks like I'm stuck here for the day," he smiles, with warmth in his eyes, something exactly like real love, and there is a scream rising in your throat. "Guess we're going to have to find something to do with our time."

If you enjoyed this story, you can discuss it with other readers and the author at the *Atropa Belladonna* story page at
http://forbiddenfiction.com/library/story/JP1-1.000050.

Deep Water Grave

Claryssa Berg

Diana is fascinated by the stories about dead sailors who are said to enter the bodies of huge, black cormorants and visit the living in that guise. One night she is visited by one of the dead men — who has come borrow her warmth.

Deep Water Grave

The locals said that dead sailors entered the bodies of the huge, black cormorants, and visited the living in that guise. Diana often watched the birds, as if looking for a sign, while she walked by the water's edge, scanning the waves keenly with her gaze, wondering what was beneath them; where the sailors had found their grave.

She had come here not long ago. Her new house was weather worn and old, overlooking the grey waves. She had come to try and find a peace of sorts. Things had not been as they should with her for a while, not since her daughter slipped from her body pale and dead. She had cried when it happened, then chosen the oblivion of tiny full moons filled with soft numbness, until her doctor told her there would be no more—then she went a little crazy. No wonder Johnny left her after that, she would have done so too...

In the dream she approached the water, longing to take a swim, though the air around her was far too cold to inspire a soak in the sea. The sky was bleak; pale grey. As were the rocks beneath her feet as she maneuvered towards the slate colored sea. He sat there, right beside her on a large rock, though she hadn't seen him there before. Curling sheets of mist around him, vapor from the sea and he said:

"Have you ever made love to a dead man?" His skin was so pale it was almost blue, and there were feathers; a thin layer of glistening black. Black as his hair, slick and wet. "You really should not..."

She was back in her bed, eyes wide open. The room was dark, and freezing. The meager light from the windows was cold like ice and moon and mirrors. And she, wrapped in her blanket: a lighthouse of warmth, an island in the sea. She gasped for air and reached for the light switch. Cold sweat of fear seeped out on her skin. She had read too much then, perhaps, about the hazards at sea. As if to make a point of it the book on her nightstand fell down and hit the carpet with a thump. *Local Legends From the Coast* was printed on the cover. She found it fascinating; disturbing. Ships and people, reality and myth, all blended together in this place. The local legends smelled of sea water, the sea water tasted of myths.

She turned on the light. Nothing happened.

How did it get so cold? A temperature drop during the night? The weather report mentioned nothing of the sort...

"Fuck." She tried the switch again, to no avail and braced herself for the chilly walk through the room to find the other lamp in the dark.

A sigh then, so soft, she barely heard it, but there it was again: a sigh. A breath of air, right by the bed.

"You dream of me, then," said a voice. "Why? Have you fallen in love with the dead?"

"No!"

He chuckled softly. "But I think you have. You call to me with this passion..."

"No." Her voice came out just a whisper.

"When you die at sea, like I did, the water is your grave. You feed it with your flesh," he said. "So cold down there, for marrow, bones... tissue coming undone... Have you ever made love to a dead man?" he asked. "Have you ever made love to the sea?"

"No..." Shivering slightly, at the verge of tears, her voice hardly carried the word.

"But will you lend me your warmth for tonight?"

She said yes. She was scared. More than scared; terrified. But who was she to deny the dead? Death had already been within her. In her *yes* was a sweet surrender.

He was cold, and moist against her skin. His fingers twined in her hair, and he kissed her, softly. Like ice, that kiss. No breath, just this: the kiss delivered on her lips. She inhaled sharply, surprised by the passion. She had not felt such cravings for some time. His hand was on her left breast, caressing it. Her nipple stood erect against his palm and goose flesh formed around the mounted peak. His skin felt slick, like fish. He kissed her again, lips lingering on lips. He tasted her: licked her chin and her neck. His hair fell into her face. Smelled like seaweeds, shells, decay. His hand kept squeezing, caressing her breast, and he slid one leg across her body, across the warm skin of her thighs.

She moaned when his lips replaced the hand on her breast and the coldness of his mouth began sucking at her skin. She held his head then, her fingers tangled in his hair, and she arched against him when he slid in place above her, between her thighs. So hot down there. His fingers between her legs were like icicles dipping into flames. She cried out. It hurt when blood-fueled fire met ice. Exquisite, that pain — pleasurable knives. Needles piercing just enough to bite. Kisses of ice — and then release, when he took his hand away.

"No," she grabbed for his fingers. "Don't..."

"So hot..." he murmured. "So warm..."

"Do it again," she begged him and pressed the cold hand to her crotch. He laughed and shrugged her hands off, shifted, repositioned himself and leaned down to touch her lips with his own. Another kiss tasting of salt and darkness. She felt his cock pressing firmly against her. A thick rod of slick flesh, searing her skin with its cold.

"Yes!"

He held one of her thighs in his hand and pushed it towards her to make more room as he slid inside. She made a yelping sound and bit into her chilled lips, closed her eyes against the pain when he entered her, swiftly, until all of him was in all of her — and she surrounded him with her hot blood flowing behind thin walls, and drenched him in salty moisture of her own. "Please..."

He made a sound deep in his throat and moved carefully above her. Hard ice burned her insides and she cried out with a mixture of pleasure and pain; clenched him hard with her muscles. Moved her hips in time with his and tangled her hands in his hair again. She felt him go faster — harder. His fingers cut into her thigh, her hip, while he forcefully took her; her warmth, her flesh.

"So warm," he murmured, "so warm..." He set up the pace, as rhythmic as the waves.

And she begged him: "please!" while she rode the waves he made in her. Water. Dark water. Deep. Black water from the grave, crashing upon her shore, making her feel alive. Slick flesh inside of her, pushing her, closer — closer, until she spilled over and came in a hard, foaming tide ...

"Yes!"

His cock twitched inside of her and she cried out his name, "Daniel!" while he came.

He went silent. "You know my name?"

"No." She did not.

He lay down heavy upon her. "But you did," he said, "you have been listening to the waves."

She said nothing then, just lay there. Her fingers caressing his temple, his jaw... her body was steadily cooling after the outburst of heat, and his weight upon her became increasingly heavier, colder, pinning her down.

Diana woke up with light filtering through the curtains: White. Pale as moonbeams. The blanket was on the floor. The room was still cold and her sheets were wet. When she staggered from the bed and passed the mirror she could see her lips had turned a shade of blue — bruised. Her teeth clattered. She went into the bathroom and turned on the shower. Hot water — searingly so. Mist rose from her skin when she stepped into the stream. She stood there for half an hour, her head resting against the tiled wall. And she thought... and she didn't — and then she cried for a while.

Her limbs were slow and sluggish when she finally turned off the water and stepped out onto the floor. She slipped into a fuzzy robe, thick and blessedly warm.

On her way through the still freezing bedroom, she tried the lights: on, off — working just fine. As they should...

She padded into the kitchen, made coffee. Did all the motions of her own morning rituals, though her heart was not in it, nor her mind.

She took her cup to the window and stared at the sea: grey as the sky. The black birds by the water's edge took flight while she poured herself another cup of coffee and she followed them with her gaze as they soared across the sky, above the silvery depths. Rippling, the ocean. Rippling with the waves. The birds circling, high above. Marking the spot. Salty grave for naked bones... The crew on that ship, lost so long ago, never made it to shore. Cormorants, soaring, crying out their pain. Spirits trapped in feathers, flesh... She touched her chest with her fingertips, chilled. Her skin was still cold — numb. She held on to her steaming cup of coffee, desperately craving its warmth. Inwardly blessing the daylight outside, her own flowing blood and strong, beating heart. Blessing the fact that she still was alive.

If you enjoyed this story, you can discuss it with other readers and the author at the *Deep Water Grave* story page at http://forbiddenfiction.com/library/story/CB1-1.000032.

Brush with Death

E.E. Grey

Dead people don't make good boyfriends. At least, that's what Grant
tries to remind himself. A painter, Grant moved into his apartment to
be alone and to work on his art, only to discover the resident ghost,
Joey. It's not all bad. Joey is a pretty good listener, a good model — and
he's hot.

Chapter 1
Not-so-invisible Roommate

It's not as if Grant actually believes in ghosts anyway.

When he tells his brother about it, Keith laughs at him, vaguely amused, and yeah. Grant is never telling anyone else about the ghost that lives in his apartment.

When he moved into the building, Grant hadn't expected anything other than a few leaky pipes, maybe the walls would need to repainted, and maybe, if it was really bad, he'd find a dead mouse in a corner. He hadn't expected to wake up one morning with a strange feeling of being watched and find that he actually *was* being watched.

Joey is the kind of ghost that Grant always pictured as the kind he'd like to live with, if he had to live with one. Which, now, he does.

He can't really explain anything about Joey, doesn't really understand anything, except that he's always there, and maybe it had freaked Grant out a little when he'd woken up that day with Joey fucking *hovering* over the bed, but he's gotten used to it. Mostly.

"Ghosts are overrated," he says when Joey drifts after him into the kitchen where he pours coffee beans in the grinder.

Joey pouts at him because he can't have any coffee. Grant finds it slightly odd that ghosts can pout, but then he finds it odd that he can talk to Joey at all.

Joey laughs at that, crossing his arms, the same impish grin on his face as always.

"You only say that because I'm here. I bet before you met me, you denied they existed."

"Didn't you?" Grant asks, because, honestly, it's true, but he doesn't tell Joey that. Joey knows him too well by now anyway. He knows exactly what Grant is thinking after all this time.

Joey shrugs, picking at the sleeve of his ripped tee shirt. Grant has never asked how he died, though he's wanted to. All he knows is that Joey has a tear in his shirt down the front, and it never goes away no matter how much Joey tries to fix it.

"I believed in zombies and vampires. How could ghosts be much different?"

Grant has to give him that one since he's pretty much completely obsessed with vampires, too. He pours himself a cup of coffee and takes a sip, Joey watching him sadly. Grant has heard enough about Joey's love of coffee to know that he misses it, possibly more than he misses sex, but Grant tries not to think about Joey and sex.

Joey, despite being dead, is a very good-looking ghost with his shaggy brown hair, big hazel eyes, and the tongue stud that Grant is sure can't actually be there. Sometimes, Grant has dreams where Joey is corporeal, and they somehow get into situations he wouldn't mind acting out if only it were real. But it's stupid and pointless and crazy, so Grant does his best not to think of Joey like that.

Joey never seems to notice the way Grant stares at his mouth, the curve of his jaw as he thinks about drawing it in one of the notebooks he's tried to keep hidden under his bed. Joey just sighs at the coffee and sweeps his transparent hand through the countertop..

"Can you see other ghosts?" Grant asks as he leaves the kitchen for his studio.

He used to think it was weird, having gotten the apartment so he could live alone and work on his art, only to find Joey and, clearly, Joey wasn't going anywhere—Grant hasn't asked about that yet either. He's not sure if he's scared to know or if it really doesn't matter. Joey never says anything.

Joey drifts after him lazily, ruffling his hair, and Grant looks away, because, like everything else with Joey, he has nice hair too.

"I've never seen any others," Joey replies vaguely. "But I don't really leave the apartment."

Grant pauses as he gets out his paints, glancing at where Joey is hovering over a stool, legs folded beneath him. He's not touching the chair. Grant has long given up trying to figure out how it works. Instead, he selects a shade of green paint from his many jars.

"Can you?"

"Can I what?" Joey asks, unfolding his legs and drifting over to peer over Grant's shoulder.

"Leave the apartment," Grant adds, turning and accidentally running into Joey, or well, stepping through him might better describe what happens. If he couldn't see Joey, he wouldn't even notice, but it's surreal as he just stumbles back. Joey hardly looks perturbed. Grant thinks that if he was real, he might be able to touch him, feel his smooth skin. Instead, he feels awkward as he maneuvers around Joey.

"Never tried," Joey replies thoughtfully. "But why bother? I don't see why anyone needs to go outside. I've got everything I need here."

His grin is as bright as the fucking sun, and sometimes, Grant wishes he did live alone so he could paint canvas after canvas of it, and Joey would never know.

Joey hovers over the stool, head tilted to the side curiously, watching Grant dip his brush in the black paint. Grant tries not to wonder how he hovers. It makes his head hurt when he tries to figure it out, and sometimes, just thinking about his art gives him a headache. That might be due to the paint, though, and not that he can never get the blood spatter right on the canvas.

He stares at Joey, brush still in his hand until he remembers he's supposed to be painting, not lusting over a ghost. Right. He's totally normal.

"Can I see it?" Joey asks eagerly, and Grant hesitates.

The painting doesn't really look like Joey, not compared to the sketches he's got tucked away where Joey can't find them. Because Joey can't touch things, so he figures hiding them in a drawer would be safe enough.

"It's not..." Grant says, awkward. This is one reason he'd rather just keep his paintings to himself, especially ones where he gets to stare at a really hot guy all day.

"Let me see," Joey insists, gliding off the chair. Grant takes a stumbling step backward, tripping over a can of paint that sends him sprawling backwards, arms flailing like a spider on its back. He hits the wall with a loud thud, stars blooming before his eyes.

"Holy shit!" Joey says, and he's there in the blink of an eye, hand hovering over Grant's face as if he wants to touch him, to make sure he's okay. "Grant? Grant?"

Grant blinks slowly; reaching back to rub his head, but there's no blood. Thank God. He might faint if there was. Joey's panicked eyes dart all over him, and Grant realizes just how close they are. Close enough to touch… if they could touch.

His cheeks flush in embarrassment and a little of something else as he tries to shift, pushing himself up.

"Do you have a concussion?" Joey demands, pressing his hands together since he can't do anything else. He reaches forward, and Grant watches his hand pass the side of his face, a ghost of a touch. He swears he can feel the breeze, but that's insane. Joey can't even sit down. He can't make air move.

Something aches deep inside Grant as he stares up at Joey. If only he were real, if only he could reach up and touch him. He shakes himself sharply, though. Joey is dead, has been for a while. Maybe he does spend too much time with his paints.

Joey doesn't stop hovering over him until he finally rises from the floor, rubbing the bump on the back of his head. He needs more coffee.

"I'm fine," he mutters, shoving his hair back and feeling like an idiot. Not that that's a new sensation. It just sucks when a ghost is worried about your safety.

If he could be any more of a loser, he would be, but Grant can't help it. He's an anti-social painter who'd rather spend his time drawing than going out in the real world. He doesn't see what's wrong with that, though he's sure Keith could make an entire list's worth of reasons.

"I'm not that fat, am I?" Joey asks, staring at the painting, eyes squinted to make out what is more or less his shape, twisted in red mist.

Grant blushes as Joey pulls up his ripped shirt to stare at his own abs. He's not fat.

Grant really does need to get out more.

"How's the ghost?" Keith is still sort of laughing at him, and Grant rues the day he ever brought it up, but it had been fucking weird the first time! He'd had to tell someone. Of course, when Keith had come over; Grant determined to prove he wasn't crazy, Keith hadn't been able to see Joey. Joey had spent all the time making fun of Keith's glasses.

Grumbling, Grant sips his coffee and tries to remind himself that it is a good thing to meet his brother at least once a week. It's mostly so Keith can be sure he hasn't died in an avalanche of canvases, and the poor neighbor won't have to find his body a week later.

"He's real," he insists, annoyed. Keith still doesn't believe him, and he might be beginning to think that Grant is losing it, shut up in his apartment with only paint fumes for company.

"Right," Keith mutters, clearly humoring him. Rolling his eyes, Grant sinks down into his chair instead. Keith pushes up his glasses, glancing at Grant. "So what time is the show next week?"

"Starts at seven," Grant mutters, thinking about the paintings stacked up in his studio, the ones that Joey actually agreed to pose for.

"And you're actually going to be there and talk to people, right?" Keith asks, arching an eyebrow behind his glasses. "Because it's your show, and sometimes people like to talk to the artist."

"Yeah, yeah," Grant mumbles. So what if he prefers to stay home? Home is nice. It's just, he needs the money. Otherwise, he'd never leave his home. Being a starving artist is all well and good until you starve to death.

Keith nods slowly. "Maybe you should bring a date."

"A date?" Grant stares. He hasn't been on a date in God knows how many months, can't remember the last time he did. He certainly hasn't been with anyone since he realized Joey could float through walls and locked doors. Things can be difficult when he just needs relief and ends up thinking about Joey. He doesn't want Joey to float in while he's got his hand shoved under his boxers. It's awkward enough to be thinking about a ghost, let alone one who could float in at any moment.

Luckily, Joey seems to understand the personal space thing pretty well, and has only surprised Grant a few times in the shower.

"Yeah, like a living, breathing person," Keith says, as if it's obvious. "You do remember what those are? Not a ghost."

Grant glares. "Yes, I know."

Keith only shrugs, reaching for the cinnamon on the table, turning it over in his hands instead of putting it in his coffee. "Just making sure you can still tell the difference."

Grant is never telling Keith anything about his life again.

Grant is always frazzled before gallery shows because people call, about framing and layout and color schemes, and he doesn't know what to tell any of them. He can't deal with people. Which is probably why he gets along with a ghost so well. Gallery shows are really more of a social anxiety fest than anything else.

His agent calls repeatedly, reminding him to actually show up, so much that he nearly throws his phone in a jar of paint, but Joey is there, whispering soothing things into his ear about how he should channel his frustration into painting, which he does, and it turns out pretty well considering it's an abstract piece about strangling a phone.

Grant doesn't like gallery shows for several reasons. Mostly, he doesn't like having to talk to people he doesn't know. He doesn't like the stress of gathering things together either, and of all things, he doesn't like being there when people critique his art. As Keith would remind him, though, and has a million times, if he wants to keep living in his ghost-filled apartment, he needs the money.

He drops a jar of red paint and cuts himself on a broken glass. He nearly faints once he figures out it's not all paint, and his hand is bleeding profusely.

"Are you okay?" Joey asks as Grant holds his hand under the

sink, head turned away and eyes squeezed closed. If he doesn't look at it, it's not real, right?

"Uhh," he says, heart pounding. "Yeah. Just... Yeah."

Joey whispers soothing words as Grant tries to bandage it up. He's not good with blood or needles, or anything like that, which is weird considering how much blood he paints. It's only one bump in the road to the gallery show, though.

"You shouldn't freak out," Joey tells him as he hovers near the studio door, away from where Grant is flinging blue paint at the canvas. It's already in his hair and covering his fingertips. He frowns as he glances over at Joey.

"Easy for you to say," he mutters. "You're dead."

Joey quirks a smile. "Wasn't always. And I know it sucks, but think of afterwards."

"When I can come back here and pretend I didn't spend a day schmoozing people who don't give a fuck about art?" Grant asks, rubbing his forehead tiredly and smearing more paint over his face.

Joey drifts over, and Grant imagines that if he could actually touch things, he might be hugging him, but as it is, he just pauses next to Grant.

"After you make a ton of money on your awesome paintings and everybody wishes they were as awesome as you," he says warmly instead, and Grant catches his smile.

"Are you actually a muse spirit or something?" he asks, and Joey grins.

"Nope, just a regular, run-of-the-mill ghost, trying to make life a little easier."

Grant raises a skeptical eyebrow, but Joey's smile doesn't falter.

"You know," Joey says, "if you died, your paintings would be worth more."

Grant frowns, turning back to the canvas. "If I died, it wouldn't matter 'cause I'd be dead." He glances at Joey. He could ask Joey how he died, and Joey might answer, but Joey is behind him, frowning slightly, something sad in his gaze, and Grant can't bring himself to ask.. He sighs instead.

"Okay, so after everyone tells me I'm awesome, what do I do?"

Joey immediately grins, and Grant almost wishes he were dead so he wouldn't have a ridiculous crush on a ghost.

There are a lot of things Grant has never asked Joey, and granted he's only know Joey for about four months, but there are things he wants to know. He wants to know what it's like to die, if it really hurts, if there's some sort of catch to coming back as a ghost. He doesn't ask, though, because as much as he wants to know, Joey doesn't ever talk about his death, and whenever Grant hints at it, he usually changes the subject.

Sometimes, late at night when Grant can't sleep, Joey will lie on the bed, as though he can almost feel the warmth of the covers. Grant's not sure what he can feel and what he can't, or if he can feel *anything*. Sometimes, Joey will stay up with him—he's not sure if Joey sleeps either—and listen to him talk about all the strange things he thinks about, like vampires and zombies, his irrational fear of spiders. Like how when he was younger, he and Keith used to play hide and seek in his grandmother's basement, how he'd gotten stuck in an old box once filled with musty clothes and they didn't find him for hours. It probably doesn't make much sense since Grant knows that Joey *is* a ghost, and he can't do anything except listen and offer his opinion, but it makes him feel less alone, and he knows it's stupid, but sometimes, he really wishes he had met Joey when Joey was alive, because he's pretty sure it would have been awesome.

As it is, Joey is transparent and spends his time drifting around the apartment aimlessly, never leaving when Grant does, and always there when he gets back.

Joey talks back too, though, tells Grant stories of when he was alive, his friends. He tells Grant he should be more careful when he crosses the street as Grant tells him of the time he nearly got run over by a bike the week before. Grant ignores that since it doesn't matter. He's not going to die anytime soon, he's pretty sure, unless a plane crashes into the side of his house, or unless Joey really is right and that would sell more paintings.

The night of the gallery show, Joey watches Grant pull on a nice jacket and jeans, forgoing the uncomfortable shoes and just wearing his paint-splattered converse instead. It's his show; he should be comfortable.

"You look awesome," Joey says, and Grant thinks he hears a hint of longing in Joey's voice, but Joey just smiles at him in the mirror. Grant wants to ask about ghosts and mirrors, but he doesn't, turning around.

"Yeah?" he asks uncertainly, ruffling his messy blond hair, trying to remember the last time he got it cut, but he can't. His shoulders are too thin for the jacket, and it hangs on his frame, like a kid playing dress-up. He doesn't like dressing up. Hell, he doesn't like dressing at all, and he'd lounge around all day in his pajamas if he *actually* lived alone.

"Yeah," Joey echoes firmly. "You're gonna sell a million paintings."

"I'm only showing forty."

Joey rolls his eyes fondly. "Same difference."

Grant doesn't correct him and sweeps his hair back uselessly, but it falls back into his eyes a second later. "Okay," he says finally. "I think I'm ready."

"Go sell those pictures," Joey says as he turns from the mirror. "And look both ways before you cross the street."

Grant doesn't ask what that means as he stuffs his wallet in his back pocket and leaves, locking the door behind him.

"You didn't bring a date."

Grant wants to scowl, but Keith is arching a knowing eyebrow as if he expected it to happen, and really, he should have. Grant never said he would bring someone. He has no one to bring anyway, and the one person he would have liked to have brought is see-through and currently hovering over his couch.

"I brought myself," he replies instead. "That's enough."

Grant is counting the hours until he can go home to Joey and tell him that it was just as bad as he'd expected.

"There you are," a woman says from behind him, clamping a hand on his shoulder and turning him around. Grant sighs as he catches sight of the long, dark purple hair of his agent.

Lindsay already has a glass in hand and ignores the way Grant's face falls. "Good to see you out and about." She nods at Keith. "How'd you manage it?"

Keith shrugs, and Lindsay turns back to Grant.

"Have you seen Aaron's new stuff? It's gorgeous. You and he should think about doing a team exhibit one of these days, branch out from your red and black palette."

Grant hates gallery shows. He'd rather just let someone else do the selling while he paints more canvases. But he needs the money. There's no denying that. He wouldn't do it with Aaron, though, the guy who always seems to out-sell him no matter what the show is.

"Look, there's a buyer who wants to talk to you," Lindsay says seriously, and Grant closes his eyes and wishes for home. "Stay here and don't sneak off."

As she leaves, Grant groans, and Keith doesn't roll his eyes but nods through the crowd at a man with short brown hair, over by one of the paintings.

"Aaron brought a new guy," he only says. "Someone from work."

"A new toy?" Grant asks dully because Aaron always seems to have one.

"Just a friend, Troy," Keith replies. "Apparently."

The short, sinewy guy with lanky brown hair standing next to Aaron looks a little bored to be honest, and Grant doesn't blame him. Art isn't for everyone, especially when they're dragged to a show against their will. Although Grant would like to think that his paintings aren't as boring as some of those impressionist artists who stick a can on a pedestal and call it art.

"You should go talk to him," Keith says, and Grant knows it's a push. He doesn't need a push, okay? He's perfectly content with the way his life is going even if he barely sees anyone other than Joey and Keith.

"I don't want to talk to him," Grant says firmly, but when Keith just shrugs and his gaze strays across the room to his friend, Luke, on the other side, he knows it's only a matter of time before there's a plan to get him and Troy together. Luke can never resist a set-up, especially when Keith asks him.

Troy isn't a bad guy, and actually, Grant kind of thinks he's pretty hot, which might explain how they end up stumbling up the stairs to his apartment, Troy's hands pawing at his belt before they even get to his hallway.

Troy pushes him up against the wall, a little rougher than Grant is used to, a dark gleam in his eyes as he tugs at Grant's belt, the clink loud in the empty hall as he gets it apart.

"Troy," Grant gasps as Troy goes for his neck, biting down hard, so hard there'll definitely be a mark the next day. Grant tries to remember that they're still in the hallway, and he may not know his neighbors very well, but he's pretty sure they'd be upset if they walked out and found him having sex in the hallway.

Troy pulls away for only a second, hands moving to the zipper on Grant's jeans and pulling the button undone.

"Aaron said you weren't adventurous, but I think he was wrong."

Grant jumps at Troy's hand shoving into his jeans, and he gropes helplessly at the doorknob to his apartment.

"Yeah," he breathes, fumbling to pull the door open as Troy returns to his neck, sucking a dark bruise against the skin.

When they finally stumble in, Grant tugs Troy in after him, breaking him away from his neck as the door slams shut. Troy doesn't seem to care, lunging at Grant as they trip over the couch, falling backwards onto it, Troy on top as he kisses Grant hard, hand digging into his jeans until Grant gasps and arches up.

"Troy," he mutters against Troy's mouth, breaking away to pant for breath and look up as Troy grins darkly, hand wrapping around his cock and stroking once.

Mouth falling open, Grant lets his head fall back against the arm of the couch, eyes closing as Troy tugs his jeans down, jerking roughly until they slide down a few inches and his hand is back, pulling his

73

cock from the confines of his pants.

"Fuck," Grant breathes, eyes fluttering open at Troy's mouth on his stomach, tongue swirling over the skin, biting his hip. Troy's fingers trail down his thighs quickly. Troy's an impatient man.

It isn't until Troy's mouth finally encloses around him that Grant sees *him*.

Joey is hovering in the doorway to the kitchen, arms crossed, eyes narrowed, and anger brimming on his face as he watches unblinkingly.

Grant's eyes widen, and he curses under his breath. "Shit."

Joey doesn't move, just stands there and watches.

Flushing with embarrassment, Grant struggles to sit up, pushing Troy off him.

"What?" Troy asks, wiping his mouth almost as an afterthought, and Grant feels a tight clench of in his gut, flushing in what might be embarrassment or shame. He's glad Troy can't see Joey because Grant is pretty sure if Joey could touch things, he'd be strangling Troy right now.

"I-I," Grant says, glancing back to where Joey's mouth is a thin line, but Joey doesn't say anything, glaring. "I can't do this."

Troy gives him a strange look. "What?"

Struggling up, Grant zips up his jeans and backs away from the couch. "Sorry, I-I just can't."

Troy still looks confused as fuck as he pushes himself up; glancing at the way Grant is obviously hard.

"I thought you were weird," he says after a minute, sweeping his lanky hair back, "but seriously? You don't want to fuck?"

Grant doesn't reply, licking his lips and feeling horribly awkward about the whole situation, especially considering Joey hasn't said a word and he looks about two seconds away from punching Troy. Or him.

When Grant doesn't say anything, Troy scoffs and rolls his eyes. "Call me if you ever get less weird," he says as he lets himself out, the door shutting behind him a little harder than it might normally.

Letting out a breath, Grant turns to Joey, but Joey has already vanished from the doorway. Grant doesn't see him the rest of the night, and he ends up taking a shower and jerking off because he *was* hard, no thanks to Troy.

He curses to himself as his hand skates over his aching cock, so hard, but it's not Troy he's thinking of as he bites back a whine, a hand propping against the wall to keep his balance. He can see Joey's thick brown hair, feel the way he might suck him off, tongue ring scraping along his cock. He shudders, bowing his head against the hot stream of water.

When he comes, Joey's face swimming in his vision, he gasps at the heat crashing over his body, the tremble in his legs as hot come coats his fingers. He lets the water wash away all evidence of his slip-up and redresses in silence, no sign of Joey anywhere.

When he crawls into bed, he can't help thinking about the look on Joey's face, tempered anger as if all he wanted to do was tear Troy's head from his body. Rolling over, he tries not to wonder what that means because, as he reminds himself for the millionth time since he moved in, Joey is dead and dead people don't make good boyfriends.

Chapter 2
Some Things Aren't Transparent

The next morning, Grant makes coffee like normal, waiting for the smell, or the sound at least, to draw Joey out of wherever he's hiding. He dawdles in the kitchen, taking his time grinding the beans, measuring it out, listening to it percolate. He doesn't know why he's so worried. Maybe because Joey has never been mad at him before. He doesn't like it.

Eventually, Joey appears in the kitchen doorway, hovering lower to the ground than normal, a flat expression on his face as though he knows what Grant is doing, trying to lure him out with coffee he can't drink.

Grant never thought having a ghost in the house could be so much trouble.

"Hey," he greets him quietly when Joey doesn't speak, just hovers in the doorway sullenly. "Joey," he says after a minute, but Joey shakes his head.

"Sorry about last night," he says, although he doesn't really sound sorry, and he isn't looking at Grant. He rakes his hair back. Grant's pretty sure that if Joey slept, he wouldn't have last night. "Didn't mean to interrupt anything."

Grant isn't sure if Joey is still mad or if he's actually apologizing. Either way, he's not sure how to reply. "Uh," he says instead while Joey shifts his weight and finally glances at him.

"How was the show?"

"Fine," Grant replies, not knowing what else to say. What else do you say to a ghost who caught you with another guy? "I sold some stuff. I didn't die. All in all, not horrible."

Joey's expression seems to harden at his words instead of alleviating the tension as Grant had hoped.

"You're meeting Keith today?" he asks instead, and Grant pauses.

"Yeah. Lunch."

Joey nods slowly. "Watch out for busses."

Grant doesn't understand why Joey keeps giving him useless warnings, but he takes it as a good sign that Joey isn't yelling at him for the night before. He knows he shouldn't feel ashamed because it's not as if Joey is really there, not like they're in some sort of relationship. Although if Grant actually pauses to think about it, they probably kind of are.

"Sure," he mutters instead. Why everything feels like a marital spat, he can't explain.

Joey doesn't say anything more, just casts him one last glance before drifting the other way.

Lunch with Keith is the same as always except that when he asks about Troy, all Grant can do is shrug and mumble a vague answer.

"But he actually liked you," Keith says like he can't believe how much of a loser Grant is, and really, it should be no surprise. They did grow up together.

Grant can't tell Keith that it got interrupted by his ghost roommate because all he'll get is a skeptical look and a resigned sigh.

Instead, he shrugs into his coffee, frowning at the bottom of the mug. He hears Keith's sigh but tries to ignore it. It isn't as though he has a particularly exciting life, and one guy wasn't going to change that.

Well, one guy who's actually alive. A dead guy on the other hand...

Keith stares at him, shaking his head, and even Grant feels a little ashamed at himself.

"Lindsay says you did well," he said after a minute, changing the subject, but it hasn't been forgotten. Keith never lets go of anything. "Sold the decapitated girl painting."

Grant shrugs. He doesn't really care what he sold or what he didn't. He doesn't paint for other people. He paints so he can get out everything he can never say. Which is probably why he's got ten paintings of a transparent Joey shrouded in black mist.

After lunch, Keith gives Grant a bemused shake of his head. "You should really try to get out more," he says as they stand on the side-walk and the light turns from red to green. "Maybe you'd have more friends than an imaginary ghost."

"He's not imaginary," Grant argues, but the woman next to him is giving him a strange look so he just scowls as Keith shrugs.

"Either way. You should go out more."

"Thanks," Grant mutters sarcastically. "Same time next week?"

Keith nods easily. "You should bring a date."

"Shut up," Grant just mumbles, turning to cross to the subway station on the other side of the street.

"Grant!" Keith calls sharply, eyes wide, a hand outstretched use-lessly when Grant steps out.

Grant stops to look back, half a second's pause. The last thing he sees is a yellow taxi screeching towards him and then everything goes dark.

Grant's head feels as though somebody took a jackhammer to it, or like that time after the New Years' party in college when he'd woken up with a hangover to end all hangovers. This isn't like a hangover, though. This is ringing and hammering and pounding all combined and he wonders where the hell he can get some extra-extra strength Tylenol.

As he sits up, he realizes he's in his apartment on the couch. The least Keith could have done was take him to the hospital because he's obviously suffered some sort of head trauma, if the throbbing pain in his temples is anything to go by.

"Grant!" Joey's voice is entirely too loud, and Grant winces in pain. Joey immediately quiets. "Oh, right."

"Right what?" Grant grumbles, wondering why his head hurts so much. The rest of him feels fine except the hems of his pants are ripped, and his shoes are more scuffed than usual.

"Your head," Joey says as though he knows the pain now pounding in his temples. "Hurts, right?"

"Yeah," Grant grumbles. "Where is the aspirin?"

Joey only smiles, and Grant thinks it's a little mean to be laughing at his pain right now.

"You don't need aspirin," Joey tells him, drifting over to the couch and hovering in a sitting position next to him. He hesitates a second before reaching out.

Grant expects his hand to go right through him like it usually does when Joey accidentally moves through him instead of around him, but this time, he can feel the press of calloused fingers against his skin, a hand on his shoulder.

"How are you—" he asks, confused and amazed since he's never been able to feel Joey before. "How did you do that?"

Joey pauses before giving him a sad look. "Grant, I hate to be the one to tell you this but...you're dead."

Grant stares. "Dead?" he echoes dimly. "What do you mean 'dead'?"

Joey pauses. "I mean you're dead, gone, worm food, dust in the wind."

Grant still stares. "What are you talking about? I can't be dead."

"Sure you can," Joey replies, moving his hand down, and Grant can feel the touch on his skin, sort of glowingly warm, and he's pretty sure ghosts don't feel warm.

"No, I'm not dead," Grant replies firmly as panic rises in his stomach, as though Joey is crazy, as though the fact that he can feel Joey is just a weird coincidence to go along with the piercing headache.

Joey just sighs. "You are. You wanna know how I know?"

Grant doesn't believe him and he scoffs, trying to climb up from the couch, but his hands don't push off the cushions at all and his legs aren't quite moving the right way.

Joey watches him struggle. "There's a reason only you can see me, you know," he says finally, and Grant glances back at him, still trying to figure out why he can't move. "Only you can see me because only people who are about to die can see ghosts."

Grant's face transforms into a disbelieving frown. "You're crazy."

"No, you're dead," Joey replies simply, taking Grant's arm and pulling him up. Grant flails for a second, but when he looks down, he sees that his feet aren't touching the floor and that's when he starts to get really scared.

"What do you mean I'm dead?" he demands, ignoring Joey's sympathetic look.

"I mean you got hit by a taxi and you died," Joey says. "I warned you."

"You warned me about busses!" Grant cries semi-hysterically. He can't possibly be dead, and if he's dead, why is he still there? Why are his feet hovering inches over the floor and why are his legs transparent? He can see the wood floor through them now. This is just wrong.

He's surprised when Joey pulls him into a hug, and it's just like he imagined it would always be, sort of warm and all-encompassing, Joey pressed against him, arms squeezing tightly.

"I'm sorry," Joey murmurs into his shirt. "I didn't want you to die. I tried to help."

Grant is still confused as fuck and none of this makes sense. He tries to calm himself down, tries to figure out exactly what's going on, and why it feels so good with Joey wrapped around him.

Swallowing, he tries to calm down. "So if I'm... dead," he says finally, forcing the word out. "Why am I still here? Shouldn't I have moved on or something?"

Joey pulls back after a second, pausing as if considering his answer. "Some people don't move on," he replies after a minute. "Sometimes they stick around for other reasons."

"I don't have a reason," Grant argues. He doesn't have anything to stick around for except maybe to tell Keith goodbye. "Oh God, Keith," he says, suddenly stricken.

"He's okay," Joey assures him. "Well, not okay, but okay enough, you know?"

"No." Grant shakes his head. "Can I see him?"

Joey hesitates. "Can you move?"

Grant tries. He can move his arms finally but his legs are a different story. With nothing to push off from, he goes nowhere.

"What's wrong?" he asks, confused, and Joey sighs.

"It takes a while to figure out," he just says. "It's like relearning how to walk."

Grant wonders why he couldn't have just moved on like a normal ghost. Groaning, he lets his arms fall limply to his sides.

"I'm dead," he says finally. "I'm dead."

Joey gives him a sad look. "Yeah, but you're still here."

"Well, what does that mean?" Grant asks, frustrated.

Joey pauses, biting his lip, and Grant bets he could feel the tongue stud now. Shaking away that thought, he tells himself that this is the exact wrong time to be thinking about Joey's piercings.

"Grant," he says finally, slowly. "I know this is probably a bad time since you just died and all, but it's not like you have anywhere to go."

Grant frowns. Even if he is dead, he doesn't want to be reminded. He just keeps thinking about Keith and his parents and his art. What is he going to do with all his art?

"I kinda wanted to tell you for a while," Joey continues, "but it was stupid 'cause I couldn't even touch you, but now that you're a ghost... well, now, it's different."

"What is?" Grant asks, confused when Joey drifts closer, and Grant really wishes he could figure out how to move on his own.

"I can touch you now," Joey says, reaching out and grazing a hand down his arm. He pauses, licking his lips. "And ghosts can't feel real warmth, but we can feel the glow from other ghosts. I can feel you now." He glances up at Grant, who's still confused, but he can feel a tingle of nerves on his skin, and he wonders if ghosts can even feel things like that. Now is not the time to be contemplating the intricacies of ghosts, however, as Joey drifts even closer and he can't move. "And I've wanted to do this pretty much since I met you."

Grant doesn't ask what because Joey is leaning in and kissing him, and Grant thinks that maybe he should die more often if he actually gets to do this with Joey.

He kisses Joey back, noticing that Joey somehow hovers higher to get their heights right, one hand twined in his hair. Joey kisses him hard, like he's wanted to do this forever and never could, which, Grant thinks, is probably true.

"Shit," Grant mutters when Joey pulls back, breathing against his bottom lip, and somehow, Grant can *feel* it, although he's pretty sure he's not supposed to be able to. He takes a shaky breath when Joey moves back, fingers loosening in his hair. He smiles slightly, licking his lips again.

"Yeah."

Grant isn't sure what he's supposed to be feeling since he just found out that he's dead, but Joey is still there, and Joey just kissed him, and Joey is giving him that look that Troy gave him the other day except there's less predatory gleam and more genuine care.

"I wanted to do that, too," he admits after a second, and Joey's smile widens.

"I knew when you died I could finally tell you, but I still didn't want you to die," he replies quietly. "Nobody really deserves to die for nothing."

Grant frowns. "Death by taxi. What a great headline."

"I'm sure Keith will think of something better to put on your headstone," Joey assures him with a nod, and Grant feels that same sinking feeling in his stomach. He wishes he could sit down, but it doesn't seem to be working. He glances sadly at the couch.

"I can't believe I'm dead," he says again. "And you knew it was gonna happen the whole time?"

Joey looks apologetic. "Whenever someone sees me, it always means they're gonna die. I can't help it. I think it's just a force of supernatural nature or something."

Rubbing his hands through his hair, Grant sighs. "But what happens?" he asks. "Is this it?"

Joey shrugs. "It's different for everyone, I guess. I don't really know. I've only known two other people like you."

"What about when you died?" Grant thinks he's allowed to ask now that he's dead too.

Joey shrugs again. "I don't know. When I died, I was kind of like, 'this is it?' and that was it. My friends came to my apartment, here actually, and cleaned out my stuff, and I couldn't talk to them at all. It sucked, but there's nothing you can do. The best thing is to just accept it. The bright side is you don't have to worry about anything anymore."

Grant doesn't really see how that helps at all, but he sighs.

Joey gives him a small smile. "Hey, it's gonna be okay. You've still got me."

Grant laughs slightly, thinking that Joey's all he's had for a while now; he just didn't realize it until it was too late.

"So the other day with Troy," he says after a minute, and Joey frowns at the memory. "Were you jealous?"

Scoffing, Joey shakes his head. "No, Troy was disgusting."

"He was pretty hot," Grant points out, but Joey's expression darkens.

"Well, you aren't the only person who lives in this apartment," he points out moodily.

"You're dead!" Grant says with an obvious look.

"Well, so are you!" Joey replies.

"Not then, I wasn't!" Grant says indignantly. "Then I was a guy who hadn't had sex in, like, a year."

"Really?" Joey asks curiously, and Grant immediately flushes.

"Yeah," he muttered finally, "and now I'm dead, right? So I guess I'm never gonna do it again."

Joey pauses, a smile tugging at the corner of his mouth. "Weren't you listening before?"

"To the part about Troy being disgusting?"

Joey shakes his head, pulling Grant closer. Grant still feels unbalanced as he drifts forward into Joey. "To the part about ghosts and mutual senses of touch." His hand wraps around Grant's arm, and he somehow maneuvers Grant down so he's hovering over the couch in a sitting position. Grant will definitely have to ask him how to do it later.

As for now, Joey is straddling him, and it doesn't even feel like they're hovering. He can feel Joey's weight on top of him, and he doesn't really want to think about the physics of this because he was never good at science or math and this surely can't make any sense.

"We can do everything other people can, but only together. Make sense?"

"No," Grant replies honestly, because it doesn't, but he kind of doesn't care when Joey leans in, placing kisses to his throat, working his way down. He can feel the scrape of his tongue stud, and he wonders how that's possible, but it doesn't matter when Joey nips at his neck, tongue sliding over the dip in his collarbone.

Joey shifts on top of him, an impression of weight over Grant, and it doesn't matter that it's more an illusion than the real thing.

"I can touch you," Joey mutters, fingers sliding under Grant's transparent shirt, rough pads gliding over his skin, and Grant *really* wishes he had met Joey when they both were alive, but this was going to have to do. "I can kiss you." The kiss he presses to Grant's neck is wet and open-mouthed, tongue slicking up his skin as he licks up to his ear, biting the lobe while Grant shifts underneath him. He won't admit that he's thought about this pretty much since he woke up that first morning and fell out of bed at the sight of Joey. "I can feel you getting hard."

Joey grins deviously, reaching down and cupping Grant through his torn jeans, and Grant groans softly. None of this even really makes sense. He's never been a logical thinker, but this is just too weird even for him.

"How —" he tries to ask, but Joey shakes his head, using his free hand to tilt Grant's head back, licking his bottom lip slowly as he presses forward with his hips.

"Stop thinking about it," he murmurs, teeth scraping over his skin as he sucks on Grant's bottom lip. "You don't need to worry about anything anymore. Death is actually a lot better than most people think."

Grant doesn't question that, although he wants to, because Joey's hand is digging into his cock, rocking forward, and he can't help but push up into the touch, thinking that — dead or not — it has been a fucking long time.

"Joey," he mutters against his mouth, tongue flicking out to lick at Joey's lip. He pushes up, needing more, *more*.

"Yeah, fuck," Joey whispers back, untangling his hand from Grant's hair to undo the zipper and shove the jeans halfway down his thighs. When Grant glances up, Joey just shrugs. "Can't take things off all the way. Doesn't work like that."

"You've had experience?" Grant asks, and he wonders who the other two ghosts Joey had met were. It must show because Joey quirks an eyebrow.

"Just because I can't breathe or eat anymore doesn't mean I don't still want to have a steak," he says. "Doesn't mean watching you get dressed doesn't make me want to fuck you so hard you'd moan my name and your neighbors would think you were crazy."

Grant sort of stares, but Joey's hand is working its way under his underwear, warm fingers wrapping around his hard prick, and he laughs finally, cheeks flushing with embarrassment.

"They already do," he admits, and Joey smiles, stretching up for a kiss that starts out slow and quick, but turns hard and dirty as Grant drags him back when he tries to pull away.

"Thought so," Joey replies, shoving Grant's underwear down and starting to stroke.

Grant doesn't care if this is real or not; it feels good, and he can't remember the last time he had a guy as hot as Joey jerking him off.

"Here," he mutters as Joey licks a line down his palm and reaches back. Grant stutters as he reaches forward for Joey's pants, pulling the button undone and shoving his hand underneath. When Joey gasps, he takes it as a good sign and wonders just how long it's been for Joey, too.

"Fuck," Joey pants, thrusting into Grant's hand while trying to keep up the pace with his own hand. His mouth presses against Grant's neck, open and hot as he pushes forward with his hips and strokes down with his hand at the same time.

Grant tries to keep focused, but things are sort of spinning when Joey's grip tightens, and he bites back a moan instead, pushing up into Joey's grip and almost stalling out on Joey until Joey grunts and thrusts forward again.

"Sorry, sorry," Grant pants, but Joey cuts him off with a kiss, mouth dragging against his, biting his bottom lip and sucking hard. He just pushes forward, thrusting into Grant's lax grip as Grant tries to keep up when Joey squeezes around his dick and he feels the sharp tightening in his stomach.

"Just... shit," Joey mumbles, jerking Grant off as quickly as he can, and Grant feels everything going fuzzy as he pulls back from the kiss, gasping for air that he can't breathe and feeling the same illusion of release except that nothing happens. He feels the tightening and release, the strength and the fulfillment but nothing happens, and Joey doesn't pull away, biting at his jaw.

Shaking himself, Grant decides not to focus on it as he smoothes his thumb down Joey's length and Joey shudders against him, a low whine caught in the back of his throat as he reaches his high and comes down slowly. It's surreal, Grant thinks, when he pulls his hand back and it's completely clean. He supposes that's what Joey meant about mutual senses.

"Fuck," Joey mutters against Grant's cheek. "That's so much better than jerking off alone."

Grant doesn't know what to say to that, so he remains silent, feeling Joey's weight sinking against him still, warm and comforting, which is nice when he starts to think about his death again. He supposes that he really shouldn't think about it, but there are things he should have done, people he should have talked to; mostly Keith.

Joey must sense what he's thinking because he wraps himself around Grant somehow, and Grant is glad there's no post-coital stickiness to ruin the moment.

"Being dead isn't so bad," Joey murmurs. "And I kinda lied. I can leave the apartment. I just didn't want to."

Grant frowns slightly, but isn't really upset that Joey lied. Maybe he could go see Keith, if he could ever figure out how to use his legs.

"How did you die?" he asks finally because he thinks he deserves to know now.

Sighing, Joey's arms tighten. "Jersey mafia."

Grant is silent for a moment before he laughs, and Joey scowls. "Shut up," he says. "It's true."

Grant tries to stop laughing, grinning at Joey now. "Seriously?"

Joey nods. "I was a waiter and I caught them doing a deal. I was a goner after that."

"Is that why you stuck around?" Grant asks finally because he can't really figure out why he's still around. He doesn't have any unfinished business.

Joey shrugs. "Who knows. The world works in mysterious ways."

"Do you think I have some other weird reason for still being here?" Grant asks after a moment, and Joey glances up at him.

"Are you a vampire or any other undead creature?"

"Not that I know of."

Joey pauses then shrugs. "Maybe it's just what's supposed to happen, being a ghost and all." He leans back against Grant, and Grant thinks that maybe this is why he's still here. Finally, he just sighs.

"Ghosts are overrated," he mutters, and Joey just laughs, holding tighter.

If you enjoyed this story, you can discuss it with other readers and the author at the *Brush with Death* story page at http://forbiddenfiction.com/library/story/EEG-1.000073.

Witch's Price

Ann Gimpel

Alone in the aftermath of a deadly avalanche in the Italian Alps, a soldier must choose between a cold death or the assistance—and lust—of a spectral apparition.

Witch's Price

"I'm having trouble with this ski." Frustrated, and half-blinded by the churning wind pushing snow under my goggles, I tugged at the stubborn binding, trying to get it to clip against my double-layer leather boot.

"Jesus Christ, Lieutenant, you are such a pain in the ass," Sven snarled over the howl of the storm as he side-stepped up to try to help me. An arresting presence, with his thickset six-foot frame, hook nose and high cheekbones, Sven Nelson was a Colonel in the Tenth Mountain Division and my commanding officer. His normally frosty blue eyes were all but obscured behind his thick goggles and his dark whiskers were a mass of icicles. I was sure my scraggly red beard probably wasn't in any better shape. Scrunching my facial muscles experimentally, I had a hard time feeling much of anything. Even the halfway-painful tugging from beard hairs frozen into clumps was missing.

"Hi, Sven," I mumbled as he chugged alongside me.

"That would be Colonel to you, son. For chrissakes, pick up your foot so I can check that binding."

"Can you take a look at my face? Think I'm getting frostbite."

Sven swiped at his goggles, clouded from his body's heat, as he inspected my face. "Maybe," he replied tersely, poking aggressively at my cheeks with a gloved finger. "Pull your mackinaw up so it covers your cheeks, like I do with mine."

"Yeah, but that makes your goggles fog and then it's hard to see."

"Stop whining, Lieutenant. Take your pick: vision or frostbite. Seems like a simple enough choice. Bending, he yanked a wire from

89

under my foot. "That was the problem. Your binding should hold now. When we stop for the night, you'll need to wind more wire around what's left to reinforce it because you've snapped one of the strands."

"Thanks," I mumbled, reluctantly shouldering my obscenely heavy pack. It made my knees ache, never mind my back. Because I was the only electrical engineer in the group—and the one who'd more-or-less designed a prototype for the communications unit we were using—I'd gotten stuck being radio-man, which meant I had to carry the unwieldy monstrosity. An extra twenty pounds or so, which meant the pack clocked in at close to eighty.

"McDonald, try to be more careful. You'll be in a world of hurt if you lose a binding, or a ski. It's damned easy to freeze to death out here. Or shatter a leg if you get tangled up in your bindings. It'd be deucedly inconvenient to have to haul you down. Probably'd mean the Jerries'd get us."

"Not the Italians?" I shot back deadpan.

"Shut up, McDonald."

I snorted, blowing snot from my perpetually running nose onto the snow. "Gee thanks, Colonel. Got any more cheery thoughts?" Unfortunately, peering at the burgeoning storm buffeting the ten of us strung out along the mountainside, I agreed with most of what he'd said.

Raised in Colorado, it had seemed exciting to sign up for the Tenth Mountain Division so I could finally get to ski in Europe. I'd been ridiculously eager to escape my desk job designing radio circuitry. Jesus, had I been a fool, and a naïve one at that. My military service—at least so far—had been nothing but drudgery. I was constantly cold, frequently hungry and, while no stranger to storm skiing, I did prefer the occasional sunny day. The friendly recruitment officer hadn't bothered to mention we wouldn't be skiing in daylight. Nah, we had to be as inconspicuous as possible, which meant skiing at night, or in hellacious storms like the one in progress.

"Look smart, McDonald," Sven shouted, his voice raspy from the cold. "We're leaving. Everyone but you has already started up. Got to get moving or we won't make tomorrow's rendezvous. We need to get over the pass before we lose the light."

"But the wind will be worse up there," I protested, forgetting I shouldn't second-guess someone who out-ranked me. "This slope has too much wind-loading as it is. With all the fresh snow, it could avalanche." My eyes watered. Strands of hair that had escaped from under my wool watch-cap whipped me in the face. Peering through them was like looking through a blood-tinged web. My grandmother always told me only witches had red hair. Even when I was a kid, I used to wonder why she took such delight in telling me that.

As I straightened my scrawny frame, I thought wistfully of the twenty pounds I'd shed since enlisting. The pack's straps bit viciously into my wasted shoulder muscles. *Should've gotten something to eat before I put the fucking pack back on.*

"That's an order, Lieutenant."

"Sir." *Shit, nearly forgot he was even here...*

"Only women worry about avalanches." Sven punched my arm, then hustled off after his troops before the rope securing him to the next man up the hill pulled him off his feet. Shocked he'd neglected to insist I tie into the rope, and hoping I'd done a better job securing the skins to my skis than I'd done with my binding, I started up the hill at an angle just steep enough to maintain contact with the snow. Too steep and I'd fall. Not steep enough and there was no point in making the effort with that goddamned pack dragging at me like a malignant growth. Just then, a particularly brutal gust of wind tore at it, threatening to dislodge me from the hill. Feeling rattled, I tucked both my poles into one hand and turned my long-handled ice axe to the self-arrest position. There was a boulder field below. A fall could kill me.

Crap! I tore at the folds of the woolen mackinaw. My face was warm—it hurt from blood returning to the frozen parts—but I was practically blind. "One step at a time," I growled, inhaling a blast of frigid air. "One step, then another. Let the mountain take care of itself..."

"Michael... Michael sweetie..."

"What? Who said that?" It sounded like a woman's voice. I stared into the murk, unable to see six inches in front of my nose.

"Michael, over here... lover." The voice was warm and rich, sounding like a sultry, over-priced whore. It reminded me of an indulgence when we'd been in Rome and I felt pricks of guilt. But, Christ, it'd been nearly a year since I'd been home. And I *was* still a man... wasn't I?

"Michael!" The voice was sharper now, more insistent. Maybe it wasn't just my battered conscience working overtime.

"Where the hell are you?" I tried looking out into the maelstrom again, but got nowhere.

"Right next to you."

Son of a bitch! There *was* someone just downhill from me. Or was there? I squinted, trying to get a better look. "Who are you? A-and, how'd you get there?" I sputtered. "It's dangerous. If I fall, I'll take you with me."

"I'm here so you *won't* fall, Michael. In fact, I'm here to make sure you get back home alive. Christa sent me."

"What?" A sudden whoosh of wind overbalanced me. I struggled to remain upright. Out of nowhere, a curious warmth prodded me from below. Realizing I couldn't split my attention, I focused on the track through the snow ahead. Had the apparition beneath me done something? Or had I imagined the blast of hot air?

"Yes," the voice continued silkily. "It *is* better if you pay attention to your feet. Christa's worried about you. She doesn't want your son to grow up without knowing you. So, she sent me." Whatever it was sounded ridiculously pleased with herself.

The climb steepened. It took all my breath and most of my concentration. It wasn't hard to ignore whatever was trying to talk to me. Likely just a high altitude hallucination. I'd gotten them before when I'd climbed in Colorado. Not enough to eat or drink, pushing myself way too hard and the thin air made for a lethal combination. Yup. That had to be it. After all, from the glimpse I'd gotten, the thing barely wore any clothing. If it were real, it would have frozen to death.

As we neared the pass, the wind strengthened, just as I'd predicted. Why'd Sven have to be such an asshole? Like he was made of liquid testosterone and expected the rest of us to have been cut from the same mold. I negotiated a tricky kick turn, possible only because of the nine who had gone before me digging a trench into the soft snow. Thank fucking Christ I wasn't tied into the rope. Skiing roped had always felt like a suicide pact. If the guy tethered to you fell, you were both done for. Roped mountaineering was like that, too. But nobody ever talked about it.

Tendrils of curiosity surfaced from time to time. I batted them back down. I found it was easier if I didn't think about whatever might be below me. I thought about my wife Christa, with her red-gold, waist-length hair and summer-blue eyes, instead. Nearly as tall as me, we looked so similar, with strong Nordic features, we'd been accused of being brother and sister, rather than husband and wife. Grandma had still been alive — barely — at our wedding. When she'd reached up to peck at Christa's cheek with withered lips, she'd cackled something about a witchy lass for her favorite boy.

Witchy indeed! Christa was a hellion in bed. She'd dragged me into the church bathroom right after our wedding, pushed me into a stall and wrapped her long legs around me, ripping the buttons off my tuxedo pants in her haste to get to my cock. Her gown was so low-cut, it had been easy to free her breasts: milky white with large red nipples. I'd suckled them until her cunt danced around me. I could still hear her breathless, panting whisper to, "Fuck me harder, damn you." My dick twitched at the memory of the heat of her surrounding me. Maybe because it had been church and felt forbidden as hell, I'd come in just a few thrusts. So had she, laughing and gasping against my hair. "It's okay," she'd grinned. "After all, we *are* married now."

Got to think about something else. My cock had hardened, pressing against my wool ski pants. No way I could stop in the middle of this avalanche-prone slope, whip it out and give it what it obviously wanted.

Trying to refocus, I called up an image of Torsten, our boy. Nearly six, he looked just like his mother. God, I missed them both so. Thinking about them made my soul ache almost unbearably. I felt really shitty about my fall from grace in Rome. If only I could gather Christa close and feel her, really feel her against me again, all heat and curves and claws. My heart, my life, resided half a world away... For a moment, I flirted with stripping off my skins and skiing, just skiing. I was done with this war. I wanted to go home. Home was down, not up. "You stupid shit," I groaned. "You can't just desert..." Something else nagged at me. I'd been trying to ignore it, but my survival instincts screamed so incessantly I had to pay attention. It was the slope. I didn't like how it felt under my skis, mushy and insubstantial.

"Michael," the voice below me came again, holding an urgent note.

Christ, there *was* someone there… Twisting my head from side to side, I searched for whoever was trying to talk to me. "Not now," I snapped. Part of me couldn't believe I was actually trying to have a conversation with a hallucination.

"Get out of the track carefully," the woman's voice instructed. "See that boulder over there? Ski to the other side. Now."

Recognizing the wisdom in those words—for all I knew, it was some weird projection from my own mind—I hastily dragged myself fifty feet to the large boulder that formed an angle with the canyon wall. Just as I scootched through the space into a small, hollow declination, I heard a crack from above, hideous and irrevocable. The slope had let go. After a moment of free-falling silence, I heard screams, mingled with the whistling screech of hundreds of tons of snow, rampaging down the steep gully where I'd been standing not two minutes before. Spindrift from the avalanche blasted through the hole I'd just crawled through. Feeling the hot prick of tears behind my eyelids, I reached up shakily and patted the boulder that had saved my life. Thank God Sven had been distracted and forgotten I wasn't tied in…

In the stillness that followed—a deafening, stupendous quiet, made all the more conspicuous by the destruction that had come before—I heard a faint whisper, "Not God."

Ears still ringing from the cacophony of the slide, I tried to get my over-burdened brain to think. *Not God?* Where had that come from? Looking around, I didn't see the thing that had been pacing me from below. "Uh, where are you?" I ventured. More silence. I must have imagined her after all. Was I missing Christa so much I'd manufactured some sort of denial out of my angst at being unfaithful, and given it form? I turned *that* idea over in my mind, finally deciding it was unlikely since, left to my own devices, I would have stayed mindlessly in the ski tracks and been swept away with all the rest.

Oh jeez, all the rest. Steadying myself against what I might find, I skied tentatively around the bottom of my sheltering rock formation so I could look up the slope. The change in the landscape was horrifying. House-sized chunks of ice littered the sixty foot wide slot canyon like prehistoric beasts dropped randomly from above. I peered upward, anxious, heart pounding against my chest, but nothing moved. There wasn't anything sticking out of all that white; no clues that anything still lived in that chaotic ruin. I heard myself panting and tasted fear, hot and metallic, as saliva flooded my mouth. Was the mountain even done sliding? Sometimes there was a second wave, or even a third, trapping those unwise enough to launch a quick rescue effort.

Vomit filled the back of my throat. Gagging, I swallowed the sickness back down, following it with a mouthful of snow. Was *anybody* still alive? It sure didn't look like it. Side-stepping back into the lee of the boulder, I unclipped my skis.

"One thing at a time," I muttered tersely. "Get yourself situated." Removing the skins, I punched each ski tail firmly into the snow so they couldn't get away. Next, I slipped my pack off my shoulders. Grappling with the upper clasps, I tried to get a firm enough grip on the radio to pull it out with my semi-frozen fingers. This particular radio was experimental in that, while I had the main unit, each man in our group had a transceiver that allowed me to talk to him. We were only supposed to use the radios in emergencies because the cold really ate into battery time, but this sure seemed to qualify. Keying in the first frequency, I called. Nothing. Fingers freezing in the bitter wind—I couldn't operate the radio with my gloves on—I kept moving the dial. Finally, on the sixth frequency, Sven's, I heard a weak response.

"McDonald?"

"Yes, it's me. How bad are you? And where?"

"I'm deep. You'll never find me. Don't even try." There was a silence. "Think both my legs are broken. Pain's excruciating if I try to move. How'd you get away?"

"Not sure. The slope felt bad to me, so I sheltered behind a boulder." I started to tell Sven about the woman, but in the end I couldn't bring myself to mention my ghostly companion. It wasn't as if she was real.

"Smart. Should have listened to you about the pass. McDonald?"

"Yeah."

"Find my wife. Tell her," his voice broke. "Tell her I love her and I'm sorry."

"Sure, Sven, of course I'll do that."

"No more talk. Don't want to use up what little air's in this pocket any faster than I have to. Besides, save those batteries. You might need them." The radio crackled and went dead.

I looked up the slope again, peering through the opening between my boulder and the canyon wall. Another noisy cascade of boulder-laced snow rolled lazily downward, splintering off the northern escarpment. Drawing in an unsteady breath, I was grateful I'd had the wisdom to not go charging up the hill into the wreckage in search of the other guys.

With little hope, I cycled through the remaining four radio frequencies, but no one else answered. Skipping the sixth channel—no point in bothering Sven again—I ran through them again, and then a third time. My fingers had gone beyond pain. They were numb. The silence ricocheted through my soul. Alone. I really was the only one left. What god, or gods, had taken it upon themselves to make me the butt of some pitiless cosmic joke?

"I told you, *not* God." The voice sounded irritated.

Jesus, it was *her* again. "What the fuck do you mean?" Either she wasn't making any sense, or I was still painfully rattled, probably both. Regardless, I was absurdly grateful for any companionship... even from a hallucination, and pissed at myself for being weak and needy.

"Never mind about that. See that narrow strip of smooth snow right below you?"

"Uh-huh."

"Ski there."

Turning towards the boulder, using it for a windbreak, I pulled a cigarette out of one of my outer pockets. The wind tugged at the flame of my lighter, but I managed to get the thing lit. Shakily, I drew smoke into my cold-seared lungs. The nicotine hit my brain, soothing in an odd, impersonal way. "How can you know that?" I asked the disembodied voice. "I don't think it's safe to ski anywhere. There was just another..."

"I... know things." She interrupted me, laughing. It was a bright, tinkling sound, strangely out-of-place in these treacherous alpine surroundings. "You haven't done so badly as all that listening to me."

I took another deep drag on the cigarette. "How did Christa send you here?" My voice sounded shrill to me. I understood how unnerved I was, both by the death that had licked at my heels, and by my miraculous escape. Never mind the impossibility of my current conversation.

"You'll have to ask her that when you see her, Michael. Let's just say she struck a bargain. She told me I'd have a hell of a time convincing you of anything."

"Okay, so now I have a guardian angel... sent by my wife." I stubbed out my smoke on the boulder as I prepared to clip into my skis and shoulder my pack. Shaking my head vigorously from side to side to clear my churning thoughts, I felt as if I'd fallen into a vortex. "You're going to ski out of this," I told myself brusquely. "You can figure out what's going on later."

"Good plan, Michael, good plan." The seductive voice laughed again. If I looked hard, I thought I saw something floating, somehow holding its own against the stiff wind, a few feet away from me.

Reaching for one of my skis, I was stopped by an unsettling thought rising up from my childhood. A great aunt of mine — grandma's sister — had dabbled in witchcraft. Well, more than dabbled. Back in about 1920, she'd come close to being the last woman in Colorado to be tried and convicted of unnatural acts. She'd fled somewhere, to avoid being jailed, when I was around five. "Was there a, uh, price for that bargain my wife struck?" I didn't like the sound of my voice. It was wavery — and scared — but I remembered about Aunt Grimelda and her prices for things.

The apparition rounded on me, becoming far more substantial. I could see her impossibly red lips and thick dark hair. *Ach! No!* I tried closing my eyes, but when I opened them again she was still there. Somehow, impossibly, this... this, ah, whatever the hell she was, was the hooker I'd hired in Rome. I was sure of it. "Was that it?" My voice cracked. My throat felt as if it was lined with ground glass. "Was... was I the price?" Maybe being buried in that avalanche would have been better. How could I face Christa with the knowledge of my infidelity standing between us?

Then another thought surfaced. A worse one. If Christa had sicced this thing on me, what was she up to back home? I felt nauseated all over again, stomach roiling, breath catching in the back of my throat.

Shit! Maybe this whole thing was nothing but a hallucination. I needed rest, food…

That impossible laughter circled me like a living thing, each peal pounding a nail into my overheated brain. "Yes, you were a *part* of my price. Christa was more than willing to offer you up if it meant keeping you alive." The apparition sucked in a deep breath, then started laughing again. "You were so easy," she chortled between gales of mirth. "Christa at least thought you'd put up *some* resistance, but all I had to do was brush past you and… well, you were just so hungry." There was a pause, then she murmured, soft and low, "I *like* my men hungry. It pleases… those I serve."

Those she serves? What the fuck did *that* mean? I tried to dredge up memories of Grimelda, but I'd been so young that not much came. As I watched, unable to tear my eyes away, the thing glided its tongue over its full lips, moistening them. When I looked at those lips I could feel them tightening around my cock in that hotel room in Rome and, in an affront to my wife, the storm and my dead companions, that same faithless cock was suddenly hot and swollen, pressing uncomfortably against the front of my trousers.

And of course, the witch-thing knew. A wraithlike hand feathered its way past my erection. The shivery heat left in its wake was so intense, and unexpected, it was all I could do not to simply wrestle the thing down into the snow, spread its legs and plunge in. "Uh-uh," she waggled a manicured finger at me. "First, you have to ski out of here." She jabbed an index finger at my chest. "I'll be at the bottom… waiting."

"Yes?" My groin throbbed, remembering the curious combination of hot and cold that had made me half-crazy in Rome.

"You can have what you want when you get there. In fact, that's my price for helping you off this mountain."

"I thought Christa already paid you." My cock got even harder, straining against the confining fabric. I knew what it wanted.

"Prices change." The laughter morphed into a cackle. Then she hesitated, face turned towards the avalanche path, brow furrowed in concentration. "Mmmmm…" she all but purred, dark eyes full of an odd longing. "Dead, all dead."

"How can you…"

"Never mind. I just do. Now, get going."

"I don't think so." For some reason, I wasn't the least bit cold anymore. I knew what I wanted. What I had to have. All the blood in my body headed due south.

"Yes?" She arched a dark eyebrow, looking appraisingly at me.

My hands scrabbled at the front of my pants. As soon as I got the buttons undone, my cock sprang out. My hand closed over it. I was so hot. It wouldn't take much. Before I could begin the strokes that would bring me over the edge, she was there, bending over me. Her mouth was hot, then cold as she ran it up and down my shaft. Just like I remembered. "No." I pulled her upward, kissing her. The faint taste of semen from my pre-come lingered on her tongue. "You this time. Not your mouth." I pushed against her, trying to get her to lie down.

She hiked up filmy skirts, then pulled herself onto me, wrapping her legs around my waist just like Christa had done that long ago day in church. My shaft sank deep into her and I groaned. I'd never felt anything so good. Or so intense. My orgasm started almost as soon as my cock was fully inside her. And I just kept on coming. Spasm after spasm shook me. Her breath plumed hot against my neck. Finally, when I was almost to the point of pain, I felt the rhythmic contractions of her cunt milking me.

"I can see why that wife of yours wants you back... Smart. But then witches usually are." She let go of me, slithering down my body. Eying me, she smiled. "We need to do that again at the bottom." She shook her finger at me in a parody of mock severity. "This does not excuse you."

Not at all sure I could do *anything* again, I just nodded. Now that the sexual heat had dissipated, I'd begun to shiver. Stuffing myself back into my pants, I buttoned up.

"Michael, sweetie," she cooed. "It really is time to leave."

I knew she was right about it being time to go—past time actually. Between the incessant wind, the unstable slope and the snow that was continuing to fall, I'd be lucky to find the relative safety of an abandoned ski resort three thousand feet below. Pulling one ski at a time out of the snow, I yanked the skins off before clipping into them. Then I slipped on my gloves and dragged the pack over so it rested between my legs. Methodically rolling the skins, I stuffed both them and the radio back into the pack. It wasn't easy because my hands were awkward from lack of feeling; and they were trembling uncontrollably. In fact, all of me was trembling. I'd never had sex like what had just happened. Guilt sparred with pleasure and knowledge that I wanted her again. Wanted her like I'd never wanted Christa.

Bowing my head and closing my eyes, I took a couple of deep, ragged breaths. *I can ski out of here,* I told myself. *I can do the same thing I've done a thousand times before. Gather up my shit, get it on my back and let the boards carry me down...* Slitting open an eye, I looked at my hands. They seemed steadier so I gripped the pack by its carry strap and swung it onto my back. Buckling in, it didn't seem nearly as heavy as it had before.

Shrugging—my soul nearly as numb as my hands—I shoved the discrepancy to a far corner of my brain. Side-slipping a few feet, I surveyed the narrow gully, choreographed a route, turned downhill and let the fall line take me.

Transcendent warmth rose up from god only knew where—more tricks from that witch-woman thing, no doubt. After a few turns, I knew my body, at least, would find safe haven. Tickling unpleasantly, at the barest edges of my awareness, I wondered dully just what sort of unholy alliance my wife had forged on the altar of my safety. Ah, Jesus, God, what would the cost of *that* be? For I knew there'd be a price. I thought about what the thing had said. Was my wife really a witch? Just like my aunt and my grandma. And if she was, what would I do about it? The whole thing was so disturbing, I nearly missed a turn. *Can't think about that now. Gotta focus.*

Glancing about, what I saw brought me to an abrupt halt. Moving off to the side, above me and below, were the glowing specters of what had been my companions. Each man was surrounded by a luminous green nimbus, tipped with reddish flame-like projections.

As I watched, they surrounded the witch-woman, driving her further and further from me, like dogs culling a sick sheep from the herd. Sven looked right at me then and spoke. His voice had a hollow sound, but it was clear enough. "She's not what you think she is, McDonald. She's not going to save you for anything except her own twisted needs. Get down off this mountain. Now. That's an order, son." There was a pause, then he added, a hint of a bitter smile playing at the edges of his mouth, "They'll furlough you since the rest of us died. Give that wife of yours a kiss. And don't forget your promise to me."

"Michael!" The thing hadn't given up. Its voice reached me on the wind as the men drove her further away. "Don't listen to him. Tell them I'm your wife's friend. Tell them I saved your life... that they're making a mistake..."

Horror filled me. I understood. Maybe not everything, but enough. I'd fucked something dead. The glamour making it look alive had faded. Bones and blackened flesh hanging from twisted sinews were all that was under her diaphanous clothing. Turning abruptly, my mind clear for the first time since the slide, I skied for all I was worth. My buddies knew; they'd recognized the woman for the sepulchral, long-dead devil's spawn she was. They were giving me a chance and I grabbed it with both hands, sucking in deep lungfuls of air as I skied like a mad thing towards freedom and maybe, just maybe—if there was anything left there—toward home.

If you enjoyed this story, you can discuss it with other readers and the author at the *Witch's Price* story page at
http://forbiddenfiction.com/library/story/AG1-1.000079

Glad Rags

Konrad Hartmann

The dark fantasy drives Sheldon—the perfectly unresponsive partner. If satisfaction is the death of desire, only death will satisfy his desire.

Glad Rags

Sheldon thought of his desire this way: that a woman be utterly and completely receptive. That he should have all of the time in the world to explore her body, to enjoy her however he wished, that he should not have to please her or wonder if she liked what he was doing—this was his ideal scenario.

He did not want to talk or be talked to. He did not want to hear her moan or comment or give praise or criticism. He wanted nothing to interfere with the ultimate enjoyment of her body and her form. He wanted the magnificent adventure of the flesh to be shared with no one.

That a dead partner should arouse him, Sheldon would have completely and utterly denied. It was aberrant, perverse. Were he to answer honestly, he would say that he simply wanted a completely unresponsive partner that showed as little sign of life as possible.

And so Sheldon first realized he yearned for something unusual when a nervous young woman drank to the point of passing out. Her name was Marissa. Marissa would never know she would be one of the first steps on Sheldon's path to realizing his fantasy. Before her, his desire had just remained a fantasy. After Marissa, he knew it could be real.

When Marissa crumpled into the pillows on Sheldon's sofa, her form took on a yielding softness that awakened something dark in the back of Sheldon's mind. As she lay still, her little purple dress riding up, her limbs akimbo on the couch, he felt his cock immediately stiffen.

It wasn't just the opportunity for sex. Sheldon had little trouble with finding that, especially the kind of sex that did not interest him.

It wasn't that she was helpless either, or that he had power over her that excited him.

Two thoughts, mainly, came to mind. The first was she would have no realization he was there or what he would be doing to her. The second thought was more troublesome for him, and it was one he tried to push down into dark waters, as though it were a slimy eel trying to climb out. It was that she looked dead.

Ten years earlier, Sheldon witnessed the aftermath of a fatal fall from an apartment balcony. In the two seconds he saw the dead woman crumpled in the bushes next to the building—just the brief glance he saw before the body was covered—the image took root in his memory. He masturbated furiously that night, thinking of her.

And then he forgot. Sheldon forgot he had seen her, or at least, he did not remember. But now, looking at Marissa, he remembered. And now he prayed, for a few precious minutes, Marissa could be that woman.

Sheldon looked at Marissa where she sat half reclined on the couch, her legs hanging off the side. He quietly pulled the coffee table away from the couch. He crouched next to Marissa. He wanted to fuck her with a drive that was both hot and cold. But he only wanted her like this, like a limp rag doll. He did not want her if she woke up. Whether she woke up struggling and enraged, or aroused and horny—either outcome would equally disappoint him.

"Marissa," Sheldon whispered.

"Marissa." Louder this time.

"Marissa!" he called, not yelling, but loud enough to wake someone from a natural sleep. At this last call, she snorted lightly. The sound bothered Sheldon, but not enough to deter him.

He put his hand on her shoulder and shook her slightly. Her breathing changed, just a bit, but she did not stir.

And so Sheldon knelt down on the floor between her legs and said a prayer. Who he prayed to, Sheldon did not know, but he said it with passion all the same.

"Please," he said, feeling his lips quiver, building to a tremor that spread through his body. He stretched out his shaking hands, flexing the muscles and them clenching them into motionless fists. "Do not let her wake up until I am finished. Let me have this moment. Let me have it now."

Sheldon pushed Marissa's dress up past her waist. A small purple thong barely covered the bump of her pussy. He lifted the crotch of the panties, and found the fabric was light and sheer and narrow enough he could simply pull it to the side.

Marissa's cunt had not a hair on it, the skin smooth and silky. Sheldon touched it, enjoyed the soft, rubbery texture of her labia between his fingertips. Her slit was wet, and he took turns sliding each finger into its moisture. He leaned in and smelled the musky scent of her vagina.

He wanted to lick her and play with the hood of her clit, making it slide back and forth. Yet, though he planned to fuck her, he feared stimulating her to the point of waking. Likewise, he wanted to undress her and expose her small firm breasts to his attention, but he mainly wanted to fuck her and avoid the disturbance undressing her might make.

Gently, Sheldon pulled her hips closer to the edge of the couch and spread her legs further. He put a pillow under his knees to place himself at the right level, and unbuckled his pants. His cock throbbed as it pointed to Marissa's pussy. As he rolled his foreskin back, Sheldon worried he might cum too soon and miss out on his game.

He took a deep breath and rolled a condom onto his cock.

Sheldon thought of the dead woman as he parted Marissa's cunt lips with the head of his penis. His hand shook, making it hard to insert into her.

He would have cum faster, had he not worried so much about waking her. All the same, he treasured his aloneness in that moment — he didn't have to share Marissa's body with Marissa. And for a few minutes Sheldon saw her laying perfectly still and imagined her chest did not rise and fall as she breathed. He concentrated on the tightness of her pussy around his organ and the quiet of the room where the only sound was that barely audible sliding in and out.

Marissa's eyes opened slightly, as those of sleepers sometimes do, and in the self-honesty preceding orgasm, he knew she looked dead, and it was *this* that made him cum, made him cum hard with every muscle tensing up, his whole body rigid.

She stirred seconds after he came, or else he would have considered a second fucking, his arousal only slightly abated. He slid the crotch of her thong back in place, and covered her with a blanket.

Sheldon slept alone in his bed. When he woke up, Marissa was gone. They never spoke again.

The evening with Marissa haunted him. He tried to repeat the experience, cautiously, with other women, but never again were circumstances just right. Inexperienced drinkers typically became sick rather than passively unconscious, and experienced drinkers typically would not fall asleep. And when he suspected the women guessed his intentions, he felt ashamed.

But the desire became obsession, and Sheldon could not walk away from the chase. He did not himself use drugs, but he did know several dealers.

He considered slipping Restoril, Versed, or another type of drug to women in order to repeat, or even improve, the experience. But the realization he was simply becoming a rapist disturbed him. He did not consider himself much of a criminal, at least not a good one, and he was correct. He knew not how to go about things, to lie easily, and to not lie awake wondering if he would be arrested. Furthermore, the idea of overdosing the women frightened him, though he suppressed a certain thrill at the same time.

Sheldon thought about another option, and that was to simply offer drugs openly to the right women. He would not give them just any drug, only the ones that produced some variation of sedation. Perhaps he could repeat the Marissa experience. But he would not sell the drugs, only give them out. It would be a free choice for both parties. And when he pursued this option, a new world opened up for him.

Sheldon found that all roads generally led to heroin. When he wanted to find a partner willing to drug themselves into a deep nod without any questions asked of his intentions, this drug was the easy choice.

These were glorious days for Sheldon. Heroin was cheap, since he wasn't using it himself. In time, he found a semi-regular group of mostly attractive women who could achieve a deathlike stupor with some degree of predictability. This became even more predictable when Sheldon learned to cut heroin with a smidgen of Rohypnol.

And he appreciated the unspoken honesty of the encounter. Each party knew just what the other wanted and each walked away temporarily satisfied. At times he found it sad for the women, in a way, but after all, he thought, he didn't make them addicted to the drug. He only offered a mutually beneficial situation.

When Sheldon's dealer friend (now Sheldon's supplier) came upon a higher grade of heroin, he warned Sheldon to cut it down with filler.

"This isn't some bullshit, Sheldon," Jeff said, covering the bag on the table with his hand, as if to stop Sheldon from picking it up. "This is hard. Close to pure. Makes the other crap seem like *oxy*." The pointer finger of his other hand stabbed the table with each word. "You wanna cut the shit out of it with the quinine, just like I showed you. Don't give this out straight. Motherfucker's eyes'll roll back and *stay* rolled back," he said. "For real. I ain't fucking with you Sheldon, pay *attention*." Jeff nodded at Sheldon for a few seconds and then slowly took his hands away from the table and sat back.

Sheldon felt high himself driving home that night with the bag nestled against him in his jacket pocket. It felt like power, like it was an explosive. He thought about the words "close to pure." In his mind, he pictured women scattered all around his living room. In the fantasy, Sheldon was naked. He went to the first woman, a young woman, a brunette who looked much like Marissa, more like Marissa as he thought about her. She had on a pink, ruffled dress, a party dress.

Sheldon tugged it from her, roughly, no need to worry about her waking up, not with the strong stuff pumping through her veins. She lay on the couch in her pink bra and panties now, and he peeled them off like he was undressing a doll. He crouched next to her, shoving his hard penis into her slack mouth, poking it into her throat enough to make her gag reflexively.

Then he was on top of her, ramming his cock between her silky cunt lips, fucking her as hard as he could, her pussy very wet, soaking into the couch.

He hooked his arms under her legs and propped them on his

shoulders, sliding himself out of her vagina, placing the head against her asshole, and ramming it in all the way with the first stroke. He did not fuck the women like this outside of his fantasies, but this was his dream and this was his Marissa.

Her soft breath bothered him, though, and he wrapped his hands around her throat, just to make her hold her breath, but his grip tightened and tightened. As his hands tightened, so did Marissa's sphincter, and in a few minutes, there was no more breathing and she lay perfectly still and Sheldon forgot about the other women.

He climbed up and, sitting on her breasts, came a huge white streak across her blue face.

The image faded, replaced with red and blue police lights. Sheldon gripped the steering wheel and whimpered. But the car drove past and Sheldon realized he sat frozen in his own car and the crotch of his slacks was wet with semen.

He drove home sweating, and clutching the bag of heroin.

Her name was Stacy. She was blond in a color so pale as to match her skin, hair pulled back in little ponytails on either side of her head. Make-up almost covered the bruise under her eye and her long sleeves almost covered up her chicken pox arms.

Sheldon had been with Stacy before. A combination of features endeared her to him, and each time he saw her, he liked to make an inventory. The paleness of her skin. The variety of cuts and bruises. The way her ribs and hips jutted out. The way she would lay still, so deathly still.

They sat in his apartment, Stacy staring at him with half-closed eyes shrouded in the smoke of the cigarettes chained together. That was part of their unspoken contract, that Sheldon would have a carton of cigarettes on his coffee table when she arrived.

Sheldon put a small bag (not his big bag) on the table, along with a bottle of quinine. He learned early on not to try to sound cool or to pretend he knew the right words to say.

"I was told that you should cut this with this," he said, pointing to the bag and then the bottle.

"And why is that, Mr. Sheldon?" Stacy slurred.

"Well. Because it's so strong. Probably stronger than you're used to," he said.

Stacy laughed, her voice hoarse, a sandpaper throat.

"Wha'chu think, I'm a fuggin' lightweight, Sheldon?" she said. Her laugh sounded almost like a cough.

"Well. You would know about these things better than me," he said. Sheldon felt something pulling inside of himself. He pushed it down and told it to be still.

He had warned her. He couldn't be blamed if she didn't listen, but he did try again.

"I really wouldn't know," Sheldon continued. "So...as long...as... you think...you're...safe..."

Stacy no longer noticed him, her cloudy eyes clearing as they only did when drugs appeared. On the table lay the kit of a nightmare junkyard doctor. In seconds she had water and heroin in the spoon and Sheldon realized she hadn't cut it at all. He wondered what his dealer would say about that.

"You probably know better than most doctors," Sheldon said.

"Hunh?" Stacy asked. "Doctors? Yeah, I'm a fuggin' doctor, Sheldon. Sometimes you just go on and on, right?"

"Maybe...do you think...," he said. Stacy no longer appeared to hear him, or even notice he was there.

Already, she was unbuttoning her shirt and casting it off, her torso a canvas with bones threatening to poke through it. Sheldon noticed that she wore a new bra, one that fit and didn't look like it was falling off her small and firm breasts. Her body was malnourished but still had shape, still had life and beauty. He looked at her and thought of the bones underneath, her shoulder blade wings, her ribcage carved ivory. Sheldon thought of the white tulips in the vase on his kitchen table, past their peak and waiting to drop their petals. Some of the other girls were already shooting up in their foot. Stacy still had a few good veins in her arms.

"I guess there are risks in everything, right?" Sheldon said, his pulse quickening.

"Um. Yeah," Stacy said.

She sat on the couch and found an angry red hole on her arm to reuse, a little crimson cloud blossoming inside the barrel. Soon she tossed her empty rig onto the table where a drop of blood beaded on the wood.

Stacy's eyelids, already heavy, collapsed under their own weight and she sunk backwards into the couch. Sheldon's erection felt almost painful as he waited, giving it a minute. The word "priapism" scrolled across his brain.

Then he undressed as though his clothing burned him. An expectation, even a hope, tried to surface in his thoughts, but he pushed this thing aside until it climbed out and stood next to him, an almost palpable presence in the room.

Her chest rose slightly and fell quickly, having little distance to travel. He slipped his hands behind her and unhooked her bra, peeling it off. He cupped her breasts in his hands, and squeezed her nipples until they flattened between thumb and forefinger, making them hard, flicking them. Kneeling on the couch next to her, he sucked them, feeling her ragged breath as he laid his hand on her ribs.

Sheldon untied her shoes and tossed them across the room. He pushed her down on the couch and lifted her legs. Then he unbuttoned her jeans, pulling them down like he was skinning an animal. He paused at the sight of her panties. Were they made for an adult? he wondered. Even for her, they looked tiny, the image of a kitten stretched tight across her vulva.

He paused to look at her, to savor her. Stacy's breath seemed so light. A mild blankness crossed Sheldon's mind. Were her fingernails a bluish color? Were they always that color?

Sheldon hooked his thumbs under Stacy's panties and slid them down and off.

Her pubic hair was dark, almost black against her off-white skin. He pushed one leg aside until it dropped, boneless, alongside the couch. He examined the folds of her vagina, her dark labia like a puffy flower.

Sheldon reached under the couch and, for the first time, ignored the condoms there, only extracting the bottle of lubricant. He drizzled some into his palm, lubing his cock and then stuffing his fingers into Stacy's pussy, probing inside her, feeling every nuance of her flesh. Something buzzed in his brain and he wondered why the lips of her mouth looked so blue? Was it her lipstick or were they always that color?

"You'll be fine," he whispered.

His cock hurt, almost itching, and feeling like the skin would split. He climbed on top of her, punching his penis into her cunt, pinning her down, fucking and fucking. He heard no breathing as he touched his ear to her lips. Still pumping into her, he felt for a pulse on the side of her neck and found none. He was sweating now, sweating hard despite the cool air conditioning and cool skin.

Sheldon clutched the back of her neck and thrust as hard as he could into her. He felt weightless, only the smooth wet grip of Stacy's cunt around his shaft. And he had to know, had to know if it was happening. If this was real.

"You're dead. You're dead," Sheldon whispered. And he felt the pressure rise as he came. He grunted and wailed, letting his cum pulse into Stacy until he collapsed, laying his full weight on top of her.

"You're mine. You're mine. You chose this. You chose me," Sheldon whispered, stroking her hair.

As Stacy's form relaxed that night, Sheldon cleaned up after her. He washed and caressed her.

"We should buy you some new clothes," he said to her as she lay on his bed. "But we don't have much time, do we? You're already getting stiff. Still, we have some time."

Sheldon looked at her. The sheet was as white as her skin. He lifted one of her legs, lifted it all the way up until the knee touched her chest. He pushed the leg aside, her joints crackling. He lifted her arm, and tucked the leg behind it. He let go, and the leg stayed in place.

He did the same with the other leg, the joint popping even louder now, and it too, stayed in place.

Sheldon lubricated his hand, and one by one, slid all of his fingers into her pussy. Further and further he pushed, until his whole hand lay trapped in the tight embrace.

He looked up at her, at her half-open eyes, at her open mouth.

Sheldon climbed up next to her, his hand still inside her, turning it as he clambered on top of her, straddling her head and facing towards her feet. He felt inside of her mouth. It surprised him with its dryness, and so he poured more lubricant into it. He pointed his erection downwards and leaned forward as he pushed it into her mouth. Her lips and teeth brushed his cock. As he fisted her cunt, he felt the resistance of Stacy's closed throat. Still he pushed in, squeezing past the muscles that clenched him almost painfully.

His head spun and he pulled his hand out from between Stacy's legs, sucking at her clitoris as he pounded into her unyielding throat. A loud pop, and he saw a bulge under the skin of one of her hip joints. He clenched her head between his thighs and came, weeping into her vagina.

"I wish...," Sheldon said, stroking Stacy's skin, running his fingertips over her ribs, "I wish that you could stay here forever." Tears ran down his cheeks.

"I wish you could stay, but they'll come looking for you. Somebody will. The other girls will talk about me.

"And you'll never be more beautiful than you are now.

"We did our best at who we are. You couldn't help what happened. And what could I do? Accidents happen. But we will make a few — more — memories before you have to leave me."

Sheldon turned on the video camera and climbed onto the bed with Stacy.

Sheldon's course of travel took him from hardware store to hardware store. Plastic tarps at one store. A saw at another. Cleaning supplies at another. In between stops, he cried as he drove.

Sheldon tried to lift Stacy gently from the bed, but her rigid form only allowed him to grip her under her arms and drag her, her heels squeaking along the hardwood floor. He dragged her into the bathroom and, when he tried to set her carefully into the tub, she fell in so that her skull thudded against the enamel.

Though rigor mortis kept her limbs straight, her dislocated hip joints allowed her to bend, so that now her upper body rested inside the tub while her stiff legs propped her ass in the air.

Sheldon struggled out of his plastic coveralls and pulled his pants down. He grabbed a jar and threw the lid aside, slathering petroleum jelly into Stacy's rectum before pressing his penis into it. It slipped in easily, though the flesh was hardening. He grabbed her hips and fucked her as hard as he could without falling over, hearing her back crackle as he leaned into her. When he came, he pressed in deep, relishing the strange feel of her ass and knowing he would never have this experience again. But it was his moment, and he knew it would always be his and his alone.

Sheldon slid out of her and slowly lifted her legs into the tub. He dressed again in his plastic coveralls and picked up a saw.

He remembered a book written by a forensic anthropologist. When disposing of a body, the author said, many people labor to cut through rigid bone. Sheldon treasured that book when he was young, keeping it alongside an anatomy book featuring cadaver photos, the edges of certain pages worn from frequent handling. Sometimes, he would line the pages of pornographic magazines up next to the photos of bodies, creating a temporary collage of the two.

One of Sheldon's stops had been to a sporting goods store, where he picked up a book about deer hunting, including a chapter on dressing game. And so Sheldon knew to cut through the joints first.

Stacy bled slower than Sheldon had expected, but when she did it never seemed to stop, a steady flow of thick, dark blood. Soon her limbs lay neatly stacked at the upper end of the tub while he severed her head. Sweat soaked his clothes inside his coveralls.

He knew he was supposed to eviscerate her first, yet something stopped his hand from doing so until her torso lay separated from the rest of her. Using a razor and scissors, he cut carefully down her belly, and then cut a horizontal intersection.

Peeling back the flaps of skin, he felt himself grow hard once more as he plunged his gloved hands into the creamy coils of her small intestines. They seemed endless as he gently began lifting them out of her belly. Impossibly smooth, like wet silk, he lifted them and let them slide through his fingers. They were darker than he expected. He thought of the anatomy textbooks, with their eggshell-colored intestine illustrations. These were more the color of uncooked sausages.

Sheldon thought of Mrs. Grosch, his eighth-grade Health class teacher. For the first time in decades, he remembered her saying that the human body contains twenty feet of small intestines and five feet of large intestines.

Quivering, Sheldon picked up a knife and cut a foot-long section out of the small intestines. He washed it out thoroughly under the tub faucet and set it down upon Stacy's naked breast while he peeled his coveralls down around his knees and dropped his pants again.

Completely erect, he stretched and tugged the length of gut down over his cock like another foreskin. Though moist and slippery, he struggled for a moment to enter it, but soon it gripped him tightly and he closed his fist around it and pumped feverishly.

Hot tears flooded his eyes. It was a gift, a new way to be with Stacy, another way to still remain with Stacy, he thought. They were close now, closer than ever before. Sheldon felt himself blending into her, as there being such a small part of her body made it easier for her to be part of himself. He knelt on the edge of the tub as he came grunting into the tube, staring down at the pile of intestines spilling out of Stacy.

Dreaming, Sheldon stared at Stacy and Marissa, both girls lying with each other in one casket. A faint smile graced the lips of each. They lay entwined in each other's arms, their hair spilling into each other's faces. Mourners filed out of the funeral home and workers began wrapping the white sheet around both of the women.

As they lowered the lid, the funeral director approached Sheldon.

"You'll be taking them home, then?" he asked Sheldon.

Sheldon felt surprise and then embarrassment, followed by something he couldn't name. Why shouldn't he take them home?

These precious forms; lifeless, beautiful things who—that—felt nothing now would be carted off, dissected, embalmed, stuffed in a metal box to liquefy in the earth within a concrete box.

"I'm not—uh—I'm not doing anything. Anything weird with them," Sheldon said.

The man nodded, frowning slightly, his lips pursed.

Sheldon stood outside now. He saw the beach in the distance. Men in coveralls loaded the casket into his car, which was now a large station wagon.

His heart pounding, Sheldon drove away quickly with the casket.

Sheldon woke, sweating, sitting up on the couch. His back ached, tired from the work of disposing of Stacy's remains and cleaning up the bathroom.

He walked quickly to the freezer and removed a plastic freezer bag from a stack of more bags. He pulled out the frozen contents and placed them in a bowl, and then put the bowl in the microwave. He pushed the defrost button.

When the intestine was thawed and warmed in the bowl, Sheldon carried it back into the living room. He turned on the DVD player, and watched as Stacy appeared on the screen, her lips slightly parted, her hands half-clenching at the empty air.

Sheldon worked his penis into the piece of intestine and stared at himself fucking Stacy on the screen. Fucking the gut in his fist, he whispered her name over and over.

Aubrey was young, just 18 when she agreed to play dead for Sheldon. She was not an addict, and she was not interested in passing out.

But for enough money, she was willing to feign death while Sheldon took his pleasure.

"On one condition," Aubrey told Sheldon. "I have a webcam set up and recording and saved online where a friend can view it. I mean, if anything weird should happen and I disappear, someone will know to look at this video. And you have to show me, *on the camera*, that you have a condom on. That's the only way I'll do this."

So for a time, the arrangement satisfied both parties, until Aubrey called him after an appointment.

"I just watched the video. What fucking kind of condom was that?!" Aubrey yelled into the phone. "Is that fucking homemade or something?!"

Sheldon swallowed hard.

"I got it from a friend," he said.

If you enjoyed this story, you can discuss it with other readers and the author at the *Glad Rags* story page at
http://forbiddenfiction.com/library/story/KH1-1.000029.

Cold Love

Ruth Black

Caroline would do anything to have her dead ex-lover back, even dance naked in a graveyard the Scottish Highlands. She gets a lot more than she bargained for.

Cold Love

As she stepped naked into the long grass, Caroline shivered. The ground under the grass was wet and freezing, the wind blew a scouring chill all over her. Every bit of her—her sides, her breasts, even her buttocks—was trembling. Her skin had turned to goose flesh, she could feel her feet sinking into the soft ground, mud squidging between her toes, the grass stalks whipping against her bare calves, stinging them. Her skin shone whitely in the moonlight, as if she was a ghost. The moon was huge in the sky, but dark clouds were starting to scud across it. Dead ahead, facing her as she stood shaking in the bitter blast, were gravestones, round tilted humps set in parallel rows up the dark hillside.

Yet, it was worth it. A chance worth trying, maybe. Or a forlorn hope. Or both.

"Do you really believe in all that nonsense?" Sandra had asked. "D'you actually think you'll be able to bring him back?"

Caroline hadn't replied. She had bowed her head and looked at her feet.

No, she didn't believe it. Not for a second. Sentimental, pop-spiritual claptrap, that was all it was. Yet, since Chris's accident, after the worst of the grief had passed and she had been able to go back to work, to pretend she was alive and among the living again, she had tried everything—séances, tarot readers, eccentric babblers who spoke of 'the other side', self-help books with their grave, manual-like tones.

As if healing after your lover's death was like fixing an engine or going to university to listen to a lecture on it.

Still, it was necessary to reach out, to long for something. Because it seemed everything in her had become as dead and cold as a corpse since the day of Chris's death two months ago. And in that cold, dead place there was nothing to believe in, nothing to hope for. No way out.

Sandra had stared at her for a long moment over her wineglass, then set it down with a click.

"I suppose if it makes you feel a bit better..." Her voice had gone gentle, almost silky. "And you and Chris did have ... *special* interests, didn't you? ... It can't do any harm. You'll just feel a bit chilly. And wet. And stupid if anyone sees you. Very stupid. Where'd you hear about it?"

It had been at the place near the Campsie Fells, where the Highlands met the Lowlands, the *Tir Na Nog* centre, the big converted mansion house where women paid for weekends away; to meet other women in groups and support each other through Neuro-Linguistic workshops, storytelling and counselling sessions. Females walking the cloisters together, taking comfort from each other and time out from the world, and from men. In the afternoon of her last day there she and the others she had met there had walked barefoot across burning coals. Caroline had heard a sizzling sound and smelt a choking stench of ash and heat, but felt nothing more than a distant warmth, and the threat of pain if she didn't keep moving her legs. A few quick strides and she was on the other side of the glowing charcoal pit. She could still do it—push against her limits! Like she used to with Chris.

Then in the afternoon there had been the Pagan. Not the bent crone of Celtic legend, but a young woman in city clothes, a dark blue leather jacket and a light blue shirt with a blue silk scarf off-centre, her dyed red hair as long as her waist. There had been the half hour group talk and then the one-to-ones.

"I sense you've suffered a loss," she'd said. Her name, she claimed, was Sorcha, and she'd studied Caroline's face closely from under her screen of crimson fringe.

Caroline had felt her mouth and cheeks twitch. Please, no more tears, no awkward silences, no more pity. She was so sick of it. The so-called Pagan had talked to someone who knew about her here in the centre, that was all there was to it.

She had stumbled out a few words about Chris and stopped, folding her arms and tightening her lips.

"Why don't you talk with him?" the Pagan woman had asked. "I mean, communicate?"

Caroline stared at her, wondering if she should just get up and walk out. Was she joking?

"No, I mean, just to see —" the young woman had said, looking away and frowning. She seemed to hesitate, then said with a rush, "You can go there, to where he's ... you know. And you dance, and you pray. And you might make him come back. But you must go sky-clad."

"Skyclad ... pray?" Caroline smiled to hide her anger, a rage that threatened to overwhelm her sometimes.

"Yes, pray .... But more importantly, dance ... and he will come back, partly as you remember him, and partly not. And only once ... or so they say. And it must be during winter. That's what I've heard. But I don't know — I've never seen it —"

Sorcha, or whatever her name was, had stopped, fumbled with something in her pocket and brought it out. A posy of something, it looked like ferns and herbs tied tightly together with white thread.

"Take this, if you want. You're supposed to use it in some way. I'm sorry — I — I've got more people to see."

Later that day Caroline had spotted her driving away, her flame hair tied up in a neat tail, upright and deadpan behind the wheel of a shiny red Vauxhall Corsa.

That was it. It was rubbish, the whole lot of it, expensive mumbo-jumbo, except that it had made Caroline feel a bit better, just as you'd expect from a costly weekend of spoiling and pampering herself.

So why, less than a week later, had she stumbled out the story to her friend with the cool long looks and her concern, that every day, in a way Caroline couldn't quite understand, seemed to grow a little more distant?

And why was she here now despite all that her friend had said, knee-deep in soaking grass and naked as the day she was born? Getting her arse wet on a freezing November night in a filthy field with just the dead for company?

She opened her hand. All the way through, as she undressed by the dry-stone dyke, stepping warily out of boots and jeans and panties, she'd kept this in her fist, the little knot of grasses that smelled so sweetly. It had been kept by her bedside at the centre and on the mantelpiece at home, the aroma drifting to her sometimes; reminding her of something, something sweet and fragrant, something that she'd lost; as if it was some kind of talisman to remind her of better times, a charm for the past, and maybe the future.

And maybe that suited this place. After all, this graveyard in Callander to the north of Glasgow, a few miles away from *Tir Na Nog*, was some kind of ancient border, wasn't it? Which was why she'd chosen to have Chris buried here, because he had loved this area, the low rolling fields and the stark line of mountains rising above them. And not just one border, but many; a flaw between languages, lowland Scots and Highland Gaelic, between cultures and religions. Weren't there legends about fairies coming and stealing away the human beings, or stealing their babies? Maybe the old spirits of kelpies and brownies and witches still lived here? Maybe some sort of good luck charm might be needed.

Caroline's feet were sinking into the quagmire. She couldn't feel them anymore. The wind was biting at her skin, scouring and scourging it and making it shake and sting. Her eyes were full of water; she was gulping in the cold fresh air, her breath struggling in her throat. The dark humped shape of Chris's headstone was dead ahead. He'd been buried, not cremated — her decision again. Somehow she had felt it was the right one. As if it respected his body, that body she had loved and which had loved her. Somehow it had felt right.

She shuddered again. The wind filling her, seeming to try to lift her, making her lungs swell and her heart pump, as if she were a sail. Time to do something. Try it or give it up, pull on her clothes and go home.

Caroline lifted her hands and waved them. She raised her left foot, stamped it flat down. Then the same with the right — stamp-slap, stamp-slap. Slimy water sprayed up, spattering the white skin of her legs, streaking her flanks. Then through the long grass around the grave she danced, feeling stupid, as awkward and daft as if her class full of grinning twelve years olds, the ones she'd taught this morning and set homework for this evening, were gathered round the wall watching their teacher make a total fool of herself. She slapped and stamped and waved her arms, tossed her head, letting the wind swirl her and her sodden hair smack her in the face. The air howled, the grasses bent, the dark churning clouds had covered the moon. How did Pagans dance? Better than this, surely. Her skin felt drenched, her body blue with the cold, wet now and shivering. She could feel her thighs and stomach flinch and shudder.

Useless, absurd — she should give up — go home —

Hadn't her days since Chris had gone, winked out in a moment, been just like this? Going through the motions, trying to do what you were meant to do, not knowing why. Everything empty, everything gone — and now another sham —

It came hurtling out the blackness, the way it always did, the grief hitting her like a train, stopping her in her tracks, taking her breath, her sight, her hearing ...

She was on her knees, sobbing brokenly in the freezing mud.

"Oh Chris— Chris— I'm so *cold*—so cold without you— Chris, I— I've been—"

Rain started to fall, thin, freezing drops that chilled her to the marrow. She felt broken in two, a crouching, naked creature.

He was beside her suddenly. She knew it, knew it as surely as if his body was with her. She could feel his warmth, the soft strength of his muscles, his skin. See in her mind's eye his feet firmly planted in the grass, his strong arms taking her, helping her up, guiding her to the dry-stone dyke.

Another part of her was shuddering at the smell, at the touch of his corruption, the half-rotted body, the worms that she knew were in his eyes and hair. She couldn't open her eyes, didn't want to see him. Even as a part of her was shrinking and drawing back, another part of her was suddenly alight, aroused. The posy of sweet herbs, she must have dropped it. She glanced back over her shoulder. It was there on the edge of his grave. But there too in her sight, though just barely on the edge of it, was Chris's half-eaten face. He was taking her, guiding her to the wall. She knew his touch, the gentle mastery of it. Yet, she knew the thing leading her was no longer Chris; it was Chris as he was now, not as he'd been then. Yet, there was the same heat in his thighs and knees that he'd always had as he pulled her face down over them.

It was only Chris who had ever smacked her like this, who knew how to, palm full force against the right cheek and then the left. Swift and accurate, slapping upwards so that each sharp spank caught her buttock and made it jump, hard enough that the smack sounded thin, the slaps stinging her bottom, making her wince and try to clench her buttocks, unable to control herself. He was finding her out the way he always had, pushing her as far as she could bear, then a little further. She could feel it warming her back there, burning her bum until the heat spread round to her thighs and hips, making it glow like a coal. More and more, harder and harder, as she gasped and wriggled her rear end.

Only Chris had ever been able to do it, to get inside her; not just her body but inside her mind, control her as surely as a rider did a horse; the smacks taking her beyond her edge, through the stinging heat of her skin and the sound of her cries and gasps and the lash of rain and stink of rotten flesh to somewhere else, somewhere sweeter.

She opened her eyes.

There was the dirty grass under her nose, and two white things dim in the darkness — her feet, beating a drumbeat on the ground in time to the echoing smacks, and two black things between those and her face, Chris's legs or what was left of them, half-eaten shreds of skin hanging off with the bone showing. A hard spank to each cheek, left and right, that seemed to drive her forward, made her lose consciousness of everything except her backside, and the fact that it was vulnerable. She gasped and arched her back. He had always had the power to do this, to make her spin, to lose herself, to draw the sharp gasps and the begging words from her mouth, to take away all her control. Suddenly she cried out more sharply. He was holding one buttock with one hand, pulling it back and spanking inside the crease, the most sensitive spot. Again only he knew how to do that, how much it hurt her and turned her on at the same time, until she couldn't stand it any more. She would have to use the safe word, the one they'd always agreed on. He would stop at once if she said it although she didn't want it to stop, but she couldn't endure it any longer, not a minute, not for a —

The stinging slaps stopped. She felt herself raised again, led somewhere. She went passively, smoulderingly, full of pride, the rain no longer chilling her through but seeming to shine on her, her bottom on fire, glowing. She was drawn to the grave, the place where he had lain until tonight, her poor mouldering lover. Caroline's arms were drawn up over her head. This was how he'd tied her when the spanking was done and they went on to their serious games. She felt something touch her softly inside one ankle. Obediently she shifted her legs apart. Always during their games he had insisted she keep her legs wide open, to emphasise her submission, her feelings of shame and embarrassment. Sometimes she'd worn a harness, sometimes he let her keep her bra on or a T-shirt, but always her arms over her head, her feet planted wide, her back upright, the classic stretched position.

Caroline could feel the grass, the wet and the mould, smell it, the mud under her feet and the rain in the air, feel it lash her shoulders. She could hear in the sky the long drawn-out rumble of thunder, close above her, but also distant, further away than the touch of him. He was moving his fingers tenderly over her, preparing her, nudging her waist, her shoulder, the small of her back to make her arch it even more. She could feel his terrifying gentleness in the way he smoothed her hair back from her face. Then she couldn't feel his hands at all — knew he was standing back looking at her, weighing his instrument in his hand. It came like a streak of lightning, a crack in the sky, the slash of the whip across her back. Low down, but still too high, around her waist, making her squirm and cry out; pain lancing round her. She felt him adjust — could remember him so many times standing like this, when she'd twist round in her bonds to see him because she loved to watch him like this, naked, his cock erect, his grey eyes concentrated, frowning, as he readjusted his balance, and pulled the hand with the whip back again.

Ah! Like fire, like burning rain, the screaming streaks across her skin, marks that were changing her. She could feel them, welts like thin rails, knots and crosses over her skin, tiny cuts and lashes all over her, flaying her from top to bottom, her whole world simply the lashing whip, and it was all too much. Caroline let go of something inside, something she had been holding back, a flood of tears or pain or grief, she didn't know which. She'd had it before she had met Chris and now she had it again, now that she had lost him, the only man who'd ever loved her the way she needed, the man who knew, her, who beat her, who owned her completely. Only he had been able to release this wall in her, break it down as if breaking through a surface, her reserve. Only he could make her arch, squirm, wiggle, beg him to stop, struggle, scream. Only he could let her know her weakness, her softness, the thing she had to disguise every day.

A flash of lighting. She felt the whip cease. She knew what would come now. His cock nudged her buttocks, the crease between them. She bent over the gravestone, feeling herself open and hot. She half-turned — eager now — caught a glimpse of it, Chris's blackened penis, wet and oozing with decay, moisture gleaming in its eye, its length crawling with maggots. She gagged as it entered her anus. The smell of death was all around her, the touch of his cold skin on her behind, but his cock was hot, and she knew that this was what had kept him alive; his desire, his passion, and it was piercing her sweetly, stretching her, making her moan, filling her completely, her mind and her body, so that she was just aware of her hot blood, the pulse in her throat, the pain in her abdomen and the fullness. She knew so well his pulsing peak as he rode towards it, the moment he'd start to groan and buck. His hot essence spurting inside her, exploding …

She was lying across an old stone, bare-arsed in the rain. He was gone. As surely as she had felt his cock inside her, she could feel his passing now, and his regret, his sadness at leaving, lingering like a mist above the grave-stones. His warmth too, a memory like a scent of his desire, hanging there a moment before the wind blew it away.

She pushed herself up. She was soaking, covered in mud, standing alone, the rain and the tears coursing down her face, gingerly touching the welts on her buttocks, running her fingers over them as if they led back to a memory, or a secret once shared.

Caroline drove through the coursing rain at a steady seventy. Up ahead, the lights of the city glowing orange over the tops of the hills. Behind her, the dark wilderness, the black place where she had been. Her hair was tied in a wet knot down her back. She moved her hips in their jeans carefully over the seat, wincing with each slight shift. She was alive again, warm and content, her skin tingling, her heart singing. She would never be cold again.

Beside her on the passenger seat, the little knot of herbs, giving off their sweet perfume.

If you enjoyed this story, you can discuss it with other readers and the author at the *Cold Love* story page at
http://forbiddenfiction.com/library/story/RB1-1.000016.

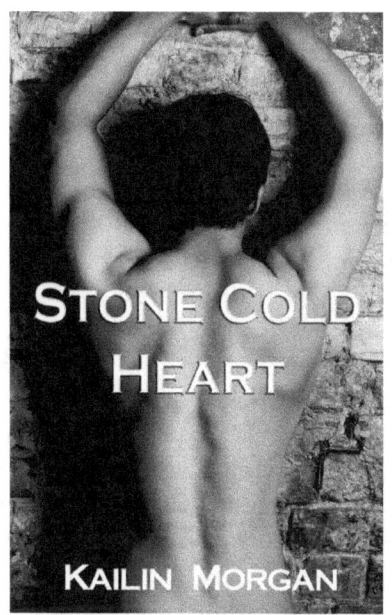

Stone Cold Heart

Kailin Morgan

Jason's got it all—good looks, nice car, his own company, staff that double as friends. When his friends persuade him to take a night out with them to enjoy himself, he never plans on risking it all to follow a stranger out into the night.

Stone Cold Heart

It's dark when I wake. It's also not my bed. Smell is the first thing I notice. The heavy scent of metal—copper and iron—stings at my nose. Underlying are the smells of damp concrete, stale piss and cigarette smoke. The floor is hard beneath me—the damp concrete. I reach out with a hand, pushing myself into a seated position, and look around, taking in the bare walls, exposed wiring and ducting on the ceiling. *Some kind of building site perhaps? Or maybe a warehouse?* I roll over to my knees, stomach protesting the change of position, cramping hard as I push myself upwards, wiping hands down my jeans.

I'm wearing jeans, so I wasn't at work. My memory is hazy, but as I move it starts coming back, flashes like strobes exposing images on a wall.

Work was finishing up. I'd just switched off my computer, was tucking some folders into my bag to look at later when Tamara, in Accounts, popped her head into my office. She rolled her eyes at the files disappearing into my bag, and told me everyone was meeting up later that evening and it was probably about time I made an appearance.

"You can't keep refusing to come out with your staff. We'll start talking about you behind your back." Her grin had been wide, teasing.

"You already talk about me behind my back." I mock-pouted, making her laugh.

"Yeah, but we'll have to start making shit up. Come on out and give us something to base our blatant lies on."

I'd laughed, then nodded my head, giving in.

The strobe flashes, shooting me forward in time, back to the present. I stumble across the concrete floor, the room—whatever it is, I'm in—lit in bands of orange from the street lights outside. My mouth feels funny, like after a bad night before, stale taste of metal. My teeth itch, feeling strange as if I'd swapped them out for someone else's. I head for a darker patch on the wall that I assume must be a door.

Lights flash again, memory stutters, and I'm in a bar, the second one of the night. Tamara is seated on the bench to my left, Sophie, my secretary, is sprawled across her lap. They're trading drinks, mouth to mouth, alcohol trickling out to be lapped up by pale pink tongues. Sophie tilts her head back, laughing at something and Tamara leans up to bite at her neck, sucking a bruise into the white skin. Sophie squeals and smacks at her shoulder.

Across the table Jason and Jeff are talking. I can't make out what they are discussing, but knowing Jason, it's probably sports. Jeff looks like he's trying to maintain his interested expression, but there's a girl I don't know perched on one of his thighs, her fingers tracing the curve of his ear, tickling down his neck. I can see Jeff's erection, pressing up against the material of his trousers, the thick line obvious, even in the dim lighting.

I can feel a body lean in against my right side, turn to see Tom, our marketing genius. We're a small company, but we're beginning to do well, and a lot of it comes down to him. I smile fondly at him and he leans in further, mouth tickling against my ear.

"I know this great club downtown, can get us in for free, know the dude that does their marketing shit. You wanna let the girls know?"

I nod and turn, tracing my finger up Tamara's spine. She squeals and spins around, almost dislodging Sophie and spilling her onto the floor.

"Tom knows this club. You want to go?" They both nod wildly.

Sophie, raising her glass, hollers a resounding, "Hell, yeah!"

Sophie moves round the table, wrapping one pale arm around Jason's neck, leaning down to speak into his ear. A thoughtful expression wanders over his face and he nods and I know he's in. Sophie must ask Jeff too, and he asks the young woman perched on his knee. Then we're all outside, attempting to summon up taxis like Pagans trying to appease the Horned God.

Strobe flashing again and I'm tripping over something, hands scraping on the cool concrete, skin abrading. I swallow the scream that jerks up my throat. I don't know if the building is empty but I don't want to attract attention, another memory tickling at the back of my mind. I need to be quiet. I twist round frantically, pulling at whatever has twined its way around my ankles. I feel fabric and tug hard. It jerks free, flopping over my chest. I bite back a small yelp of surprise and then a nervous giggle jerks out of me, loud in the quiet room, as I recognise my coat.

I smooth the fabric out with my palms, then turn them over in the dim light. I could swear I felt them scrape hard on the floor, but the skin is unbroken, even and whole in the orange glow. I stagger back to my feet, breath sighing out of me with the release of tension, stomach clenching with hunger. Sliding my coat on, more out of habit than need, the smell of perfume and sweat drifts up to my nose. I blink and time spins again.

We're in the club; Sophie and Tamara are already up dancing, arms rising above their heads, hips rocking sinuously to the beat. Jeff and his mystery lady have found a seat and he's got his hand splayed wide across the small of her back, fingers working under the fabric of her top. Her fingers are twisting in the curls at the nape of his neck, her mouth pink and moist where he's kissed away her lipstick.

Jason places a hand on my shoulder to get my attention and, when I look at him, he nods in the direction of two women sitting on the far side of the dance floor. They're pretty enough, one all blonde and long tan limbs, the other dark-haired, coffee-skinned. The brunette notices our gaze, curves plush lips into a smile. I give Jason a slight push as I shake my head in refusal. I can see her shrug but she turns her dark gaze straight to Jason and he's heading across the room without a word of farewell.

Tom's body presses against my spine, one arm moving round in front of my face, bearing a shot glass. I twist slightly so I can see his face, his blue eyes glazed with liquor and pupils wide. I grin and take the drink, tipping it back in one long swallow.

The alcohol burns pleasantly and Tom's muscled forearm is resting warm and heavy over my shoulder, his hand against my chest. He leans into me again, chin dropping to my shoulder as he places his mouth against my ear.

"Dude over there, back corner. Cannot take his eyes off you, man!

Been staring at you since you came in."

I glance over and then look back. I try not to stare. I can't believe someone like that is looking at me. I know I'm not ugly, but this guy should be in those adverts where they have some impossibly pretty man looking so delicious that it takes you minutes to work out what the product is. Dark eyes above high cheekbones, a softly pouted mouth that curves into a small smirk as he notices my attention.

His hair is dark, tousled into soft spikes, making his skin look even fairer than it probably is. He's much smaller than Tom, his body slender, but I can see the strong lines of muscle in his arms, exposed by the vest he's wearing.

I can feel the hard planes of Tom's body behind me, the firming line of his cock, where his hips press up against my ass. I tilt my head back, leaning it on his shoulder so that I can talk into his ear, the music pulsing loud around us.

"Sure it's not you he's looking at?"

"Nuh-uh. I went off to the bar and he was definitely checking you out. You gonna go over?"

"You don't mind?"

"Nah. I mean, I like what we do, but we both know it's just a casual thing, something to take the edge off once in a while. Plus, I'm gonna see if I can get tall, bald and gorgeous over there to blow me in the bathroom."

I follow Tom's wave, see who he means. You can't miss him; nearly as tall as Tom, his shaved head glistening slightly under the flashing lights. Strong and muscled, he's definitely Tom's type. But he also looks pretty straight, judging by the way his eyes keep dropping to the cleavage of the woman in front of him.

"Good luck, man. Think you'll need it more than me." Tom just laughs, head thrown back and strolls over. I turn back to the corner, but the dark-haired man has gone. "Fuck!" I curse lowly.

"Here or outside?" The voice pours into my ear on a cool breath and I turn slowly to see him behind me. An eyebrow quirks upward and that smirk appears again. Arousal stutters through me and then I'm following him outside. I can't believe I'm doing it. One-night pickups have never been my thing. I'm only sleeping with Tom, because, well for one he's hot as the sun, and two, I've known him for years, knew that he would be safe.

But then we're out in the street, the soft sounds of traffic soothing after the pulsing bass of the club. The air is chill and I wonder vaguely why the man in front of me doesn't seem to feel it, his pale skin smooth. He grins at me, teeth bright and sharp. I blink, and it's just a normal grin. I knew that last shot was one too many. But cool fingers are wrapping round my wrist and he's tugging me after him, down the alley at the side of the club, across the street and into the shell of a building under construction.

The chill in the air clears my mind and I pull back against his grip.

"Look, not here. Why don't we go back to the club? I don't do this kind of..."

Suddenly, I'm spinning round. I stagger, dizzy, back hitting against the bare plaster of a wall. He's so close; I can see flecks of gold in his green eyes. Dark lashes flicker down as his gaze drops to my mouth and I can't help running my tongue over my lips. He grins again, another flash of teeth that seem to be too many and too sharp. He's leaning into me, chest to chest. I try to push him away but he holds me up against the wall, muscles barely bunching.

"Mine." His voice is low, almost feral and I shiver; can't tell if it's fear or desire.

My pulse races and I can feel my cheeks flush as he slides cool fingers down the sides of my neck, tucking them under the collar of my jacket, sliding fabric down my arms. It slips free and he throws it carelessly somewhere behind him.

"Hey, watch my..." My voice trails off on a moan as his fingers slide back up, this time over the cotton of the t-shirt I'm wearing. He smiles up at me from under those long lashes, running a nail over the nipple that has already pebbled in the chill air. His hips move in and he grinds against me, a long slow roll of motion that flexes his body like a wave.

Any thoughts of heading back to the club disappear in the slow burn of heat and lust as his fingers tangle into my hair, holding me steady for his mouth. His lips are cool against mine, parting slowly as his tongue slips out, tracing my bottom lip, slicking it up. He bites gently and I moan, opening my mouth to his tongue.

Hands trace down my arms, wrap around my wrists and then slowly slide back up, taking my arms with them until my hands are up above my head. His tongue slips deeper into my mouth, tracing over teeth, pushing against the roof of my mouth and then tangling around mine. I try to pull away from him, needing air; hearing the soft gasps that echo quietly in the empty space. I realise they're mine.

His hips grind against mine again, applying pressure in just the right spot to make my eyes close and my head fall back against the wall. I don't even notice his hands leave my wrists until they return. I feel something twist against and around them and I lift my head to stare at him. He meets my stare with a smirk and I tilt my head back and to the side as I try to pull my arms down.

"What the fuck?" My wrists are bound with some of the trailing wires hanging from the roof space. Panic flares, bright and fast. I pull hard but it just tightens the knot, abrading my wrists, skin dampening with trickles of blood and serum.

"C'mon, man. I'm not into that kind of stuff. Just let me go."

He shakes his head and runs his hands back over my nipples, tormenting the tender flesh. My body jerks as heat flares through me, my dick swelling further, pushing awkwardly against denim.

"I don't think you have a problem with this at all." His hands slide under the hem of my t-shirt, pushing it up, shoving at it until it slides above my head, another restraint tangled around my arms. I kick out, but he's quick, moving to the side and then back. I struggle again, biceps flexing under the shirt, cursing wildly.

"C'mon, let me the fuck *go!* My friends are just across the road. Go find someone else to play your sick games with."

"No. I'm hungry and I want you. The more you struggle, the more it's going to hurt, you know." He arches his hips up against mine, friction pulling a soft gasp from me before he pulls away again. "I'm going to have you, and you won't mind at all when I'm finished." He sounds so sure of himself, eyes lit up, tongue licking over those plush lips. A chill shivers through me at the dark confidence in those eyes. They seem to grow brighter, the gold flecks flaring even more. I try to dredge up my anger.

"Why don't you take your inflated fucking ego and —"

His hand lashes out, catching my left cheek, sending my head knocking against the wall. I groan, tasting blood where I bit the inside of my mouth.

"I think we can stop with the verbal foreplay now. I'm just about good to go." His voice has gone deep and dark and despite my good intentions, it sends another shiver through me, half fear, half lust. I blink hazily and see his dark head lower to my chest. A cool mouth settles over a nipple, tongue flickering against the sensitive flesh and a little part of me whispers to just give in and enjoy it.

The chill touch of his mouth moves over the heated skin of my chest, fingers following behind it, leaving trails of goose bumps. The fingers move down, my stomach muscles contracting at the almost ticklish sensation. I can feel them trace a line along the edge of my belt before they're opening the buckle and then the button and zip give way before them.

He stops, lips curling in a smile against the skin of my stomach. He looks up at me through thick lashes and changes direction, his mouth moving upwards, teeth and tongue tracing over my collarbone, up along the pulse in my neck, fastening on to a spot behind my ear that has a gasp ripping out of me, my hips jerking against him.

He pulls back, slides a finger into my mouth, pokes at my inner cheek. A faint metallic tang follows his finger as he pulls it from my lips, coated in pink saliva, coloured by the blood I can still taste. His pink tongue flickers out, licks at the finger and he moans gently. Dark eyes, all pupil surrounded by the thinnest ring of green, fix on my mouth.

"Knew you'd taste good. I'm going to eat you up and fuck you so hard. And you want it."

I shake my head, try to deny the signals my desperate body is sending. "No! No, I don't do this. Don't want this." He laughs and spins me round; pushes my face into the wall. His hands move above me and suddenly the wire around my wrists is looser. I try to jerk away but he anticipates the movement, pulling my hips back, forcing a knee between my thighs, knocking my legs apart. The wire pulls taut again as I struggle to keep my balance.

Hands move around to the front of my hips, tugging at my jeans and then the material is being pulled down, cold air sending a trail of shivers up and down my spine. An image flashes against the back of my eyes—a man, face pressed up against a wall, hands raised and bound above his head, hips thrust out behind him, ass exposed. That's what I look like. At the same time the image manages to be almost insanely hot and also deeply humiliating.

I struggle again, but then my body stills as a hand cracks down hard across the top of a thigh, flesh stinging and blushing beneath the blow.

"I warned you. The more you fight me, the more it will hurt. I don't care if you hurt."

He uses the surprise and my sudden compliance to slide my jeans off one limb, knocking my legs apart again once he's done so. Hard, cold fingers wrap around my hips and then his chill mouth is against the base of my spine, moving downwards. I feel one hand lift off and before I can wonder where it's gone, a finger shoves hard inside me. I can feel my body clench around the intrusion and then it's pulling out, sharp nail catching at the tender skin. It stings and I can feel the soft trickle of blood, shockingly warm against my skin. Tears I hadn't noticed are trickling down my face, dropping to speckle the concrete below me.

His finger thrusts in again and I bite back a scream as it moves inside me. It's so cold and for a brief moment my mind trails off on a tangent, trying to remember the name of the syndrome that causes you to have poor circulation in your hands and feet. I jerk back to reality as his mouth joins his fingers, tongue lapping at my insides. My cock stirs again.

It had gone limp and the sudden rush of blood has my hips thrusting back against the intrusive touch. I hear him moan happily and then he's pulling his mouth away, moving up and round to my side, one finger still sliding lazy and slow inside me as he leans in. His other hand grips my chin, pulling my head round to his and he kisses me again, tongue thrusting in, tasting of blood—my blood, and other darker things.

He bites at my mouth, teeth sharp, breaking the swollen, tender skin. His tongue laps against my lips, tracing each red droplet as it wells up until I'm gasping into his mouth, hips rocking back against the slow slide of his finger. It twists inside me as he drags himself away from my bruised and swollen lips, pushing against my prostate and I shudder, body arching into the pressure, seeking more.

A soft laugh almost covers the sound of his buckle opening, a zipper sliding down. His finger pulls out and I feel his cock nudge against my hip.

"No, you can't! Not so soon. And, oh God, you need a condom. Please, please..." I struggle as much as my bonds allow, trying to tuck my hips in and away from the pressure behind me.

Fingers wrap tight around my hip, holding me steady as he ignores my plea. He shifts, then thrusts hard, pushing into me in one long steady movement. I scream against the intrusion, feel my skin tear again, blood spreading hot against his cock. He feels so cold inside me, like marble rather than flesh. I can hear him moan behind me as he slides out and back in, his thrusts eased by the slick of blood.

Chilled fingers wrap around my dick, coaxing the flaccid flesh away from my thigh. The pain and fear made me limp, but his fingers tease and caress, pulling at my cock in long slow glides that match the thrust of his hips behind me. I feel it swell once more, tears falling again as my body betrays me. I become more aware of my heat against his coolness as his body leans over mine. My pulse speeds again, my body reacting to the way he shoves against my insides, the way his hand glides over the head of my cock, rubbing against the nerves just below the head, slicking the pre-come down the length of it.

He's pushing harder and harder into me, my head lolling between my shoulders as I push back against him. I can feel my orgasm gathering as he grinds in deep, hand moving tight and fast over my dick. He sinks his teeth into my shoulder, a sharp, sun-bright flare of pain. He brings both hands to my hips, leaving my cock to jerk against my stomach as he thrusts impossibly hard, hands so tight around my hips he's almost lifting my feet from the floor. I can vaguely feel his tongue moving against my shoulder in slow laps, mouth sucking hard against the abused skin.

Ice floods through me as I feel his fluids pulse deep inside; freezing spurts mixing with the warm slick of blood as his dick spasms. He circles his hips, pushing deep and wraps his hand round my neglected cock. Then I'm coming hard on a hoarse shout, my mind blanking in a fuzz of static.

I blink again, alone in the shell of the building.

I run a hand under my t-shirt, tucking it under the other arm, pushing my fingers against the skin below my shoulder. I can feel raised marks, a group of scars in two semi-circles. Hunger cramps my belly and my interest in the scar trails off like the dust swirling in the orange glow of the street lights.

I wrap my coat tight around myself; it's cold out here in the dark as I trail out across the road, back towards the club. Music is still thumping as I slide through the doors on a nod from the bouncer. I wind my way through the mass of bodies on the dance floor, the heat sudden and shocking. My stomach clenches again, hunger knotting hard and fast.

All I can smell is sweat and perfume hanging thick over the soft tang of rust and copper. The air pulses around me, bass and heartbeats and then a soft body presses against me. I look down into Tamara's face, her eyes hazy with alcohol, cheeks flushed, skin glistening with sweat.

I wrap an arm around her, pull her in tight, burying my mouth against the warm skin of her neck. I hear her soft gasp of surprise as I walk her backwards into a dim corner.

She slurs vaguely, "Always thought you were gay."

I nod my head against her. "Don't want to fuck you, just cold, and you're so warm."

I tangle my hand into her hair, tipping her head to the side so I can trace the line of her neck with my tongue. She's so hot and I'm so hungry.

If you enjoyed this story, you can discuss it with other readers and the author at the *Stone Cold Heart* story page at
http://forbiddenfiction.com/library/story/KM1-1.000017.

The Charge of the Soul

Peter Tupper

Charlotte, the lone survivor of an undead apocalypse, finds a zombie that's different from all the others. Is it courage or loneliness that makes her believe there is more there?

Chapter 1
Alone Far in the Wilds

The sun had shone all week, so the solar cells on the roof had charged up the batteries and Charlotte decided to treat herself; her yellowed, dog-eared, water-damaged copy of *Delta of Venus*, and her vibrator, miraculously still operating after years.

Before she even got to the parts she liked, she heard the sound of cans rattling outside the lodge. Charlotte immediately clicked off the vibe, got up from bed, cinched her bathrobe, and went out onto the balcony. She scanned the perimeter fence with the binoculars, a hundred meters away from the tree-line.

A stiff had somehow gotten through, jostling the cans on the barbed wire, and now shuffled towards Charlotte's home, its motions slow and halting like its joints were rusty hinges.

"Shit, just when I try to get off..." she muttered to herself as she walked down the stairs to the hunting lodge's ground floor. It was a two-storey post and beam structure about a thirty-minute drive on a dirt road from the main road, with rocky terrain in the back and pine forest on the other sides.

Charlotte stepped into her outside boots, picked up the twelve-gauge from the gun rack next to the front door, and pumped a shell into the chamber, though it made her bad hand throb. No point using rifle rounds that were better saved for hunting. She cranked the steel door open, and stepped outside.

The stiff was halfway between the fence and the house, slowly shuffling across the weeds and grass. A bit of the barbed wire perimeter fence was tangled around one leg, scraping its skin open with every jerking step.

Charlotte walked past her parked pickup and her chicken coop and continued on a path to intercept the stiff. She kept scanning the tree-line, in case this stiff wasn't alone; they had a kind of herding instinct or reflex.

It had just passed the faded SOS sign she had painted on the ground.

Just another stiff, she thought. Funny how what was terrifying in groups was kind of pathetic individually. In a strange way, she welcomed it. It had been a long time since anything had disturbed the lodge. It would be nice to know she still had what it took.

When she was about four metres away from the stiff, she stopped and remembered the old days when the most important thing in the world to know was, *"Always go for the head shot."*

It made weird sounds as it shuffled towards her, as stiffs sometimes did, when whatever tiny shreds that remained of their former intelligence flickered on and off. *Duh...duh...duh...*

Charlotte braced the shotgun against her shoulder, sighted on the stiff's collarbone to compensate for recoil, and put her finger on the trigger.

Duh...don't...

Charlotte froze in mid-squeeze. "What the fuck...?"

"D-don't..." it said.

People used to ask Charlotte why she didn't call them "zombies, like in the movies." She always said, "Because this isn't the movies, and if we assume they only act like movie zombies, we won't adapt when they do something unexpected."

Charlotte let the gun droop. She took a good, hard look at the stiff: male, a head taller than her, dull sunken white eyes, wearing tattered rags that might have been dress pants and a shirt ages ago, bare feet because it had worn its shoes down to nothing with walking, skin encrusted with years of dirt and grime. This one was remarkably well-preserved, no missing parts or open wounds or train of intestines dragging on the ground.

Charlotte had seen stiffs missing so many parts she had no idea how they kept moving. Stiffs didn't decay the way a normal corpse did. Whatever made a human being into a stiff kept it roughly intact, just enough to shuffle around and attack humans to spread the disease. That was all they did. They never, *ever*, not once in all the years since the world fell apart, spoke even a single word.

Charlotte shook her head. The isolation was making her hear things. She raised the gun again.

"Don't..."

Charlotte stopped again. As if that wasn't strange enough, the stiff had stopped walking. The second most important thing in the world to know was, "*They always move towards you.*"

Not only was it standing still, it was actually *looking* at her, not just staring at her vaguely. Charlotte moved the shotgun back and forth and watched the stiff track it.

Keeping the stiff in full view, Charlotte circled around behind him. The stiff turned to keep watching her. She bent down, grabbed the strand of barbed wire and flicked it. After a few tries, she got it off the stiff's leg.

Still keeping a close eye on the stiff, she backed into the house and locked the front door behind her.

Charlotte sat in the lodge's radio room, sipping a cup of pine needle tea to settle her nerves.

"He talks," she said into the microphone. "And I don't mean just parroting words either, I mean actually responding to questions." It had been a long time since she had picked up anything on the lodge's radio setup. Even those weird stations that carried nothing but people reciting numbers had gone silent. Still, Charlotte kept up her broadcasts on a regular basis. Well, semi-regular.

She took another sip of tea and picked up the microphone again. "Maybe this is just me sitting in a pool of my own piss, gibbering to myself. Maybe this is the last living person on Earth talking to nobody and it doesn't matter.

"But this is something we can't ignore. I realize that, if you're listening to this, you've spent years shooting every stiff you see. But if there's one like him, stands to reason there are more. So maybe don't shoot them all on sight. I'll be broadcasting as events develop."

She set the system to repeat the message on every frequency, then walked downstairs, picked up the shotgun, unlocked the door and walked out on the lodge's porch where the stiff stood.

To be this close to a stiff, and not trying to run away or shoot it, was going against years of survival habits. Then again, this wasn't your typical stiff. Or maybe it was the fact Charlotte hadn't seen another live human being in more than a year, and this was close to it as she thought she would get.

A long time ago, people called her a social butterfly, always the life of the party, the matchmaker, the one who bought the cake when it was somebody's birthday at the office. After a couple of marriages that didn't last two years and no kids, she preferred the life of friends and dating to family.

Then one night it all changed. Her life became a never-ending stream of running, hiding, scavenging and fighting, while the stiffs came in countless waves. That was what got to her about how the world had changed; the loneliness, the lack of human contact. The fear of everyone, not just the stiffs. She bounced around from one band of survivors to another, but they always fell apart into their own savagery. In her mind, people almost became a greater threat than the stiffs, which at least were predictable. She had been on her own ever since, travelling and scavenging and avoiding other survivors until she realized she hadn't seen a sign of any others for months. No airplanes, no radio signals, no other signs of human life.

The last time she left the lodge, she drove her pickup truck on a supply mission into the crumbling remains of the city, and found it overrun with stiffs, endlessly prowling through the streets and alleys. Her luck nearly ran out when the stiffs swarmed her truck and she had to abandon it. After a terrifying night of creeping through the unlit rubble, avoiding the stiffs, she managed to fuel and hotwire another truck and drive out. After that, she stayed at the lodge, apart from a few hunting or trapping trips into the woods, living on preserved food and a few attempts at farming and raising chickens.

Charlotte dropped into the porch's rocking chair, shotgun across her lap, careful to keep the stiff in full view.

It— he? — slowly turned to look at her, dull eyes in a face covered with grime and framed with lank hair.

"Do you understand me?" Charlotte asked.

After a long time, he said, "Yes." His voice had a liquid quality, like trying to talk with a badly congested throat.

"Do you remember anything from before?"

After an even longer pause, he said, "Walking."

"So, what brings you here?" She put the cup of tea on the porch handrail. "Gonna eat me?" Charlotte realized she was mainly talking to herself and not the stiff, but that was hardly news after years of isolation. Arguably, this was *more* sane than talking to herself. She remembered some old movie about a guy living alone in a city who set up mannequins to talk to, but she swore she'd never be that pathetic. So she talked to the squirrels that picked up crumbs on the porch, to the crows that perched on the perimeter fences, to the people in her hoard of DVDs, to the walls.

"You're the only stiff I've ever seen who didn't try to eat my face. Just so you know, I feel a certain obligation to stay alive, if only for historical value. I am, so far as I know, the sole survivor of a great civilization, keeper of the lost secrets like silly string and pornography.

"You know what that means? I might just be the last human being alive. Everybody else is dead, or like you. Except not as chatty." She spread her arms wide. "Take a good look, last chance to see an endangered species. And you know who endangered me? You did. All you stiffs. Stupid, shuffling, moaning, dirty stiffs. Fuck, insects are more alive than you. I've put down over a thousand stiffs over the years. Got pretty good at it, too." Knowing it was the wrong thing, but not caring enough, she raised the gun to aim it at him.

"Don't..." He took a halting step back and bumped against the porch railing.

"I also killed about twenty people. They talked too." That brought up bad memories.

"Don't... please..." he said.

"You're begging for your life. Maybe that means you're alive, somehow." She put the gun down again. "You got a name?"

Another pause. He said, "No...?"

"Well, I'm not naming you 'Adam.'" Charlotte looked at him for a while. "You're Max," she said. "My mama had a cat named Max once, and that's a good a name as any."

"Ma... Ma-ks... Max."

"Yeah, Max the talking stiff. I'm Charlotte."

"Shar-ut..."

Charlotte jerked back and raised the shotgun as Max took lurching steps across the porch, but not towards her. She let the gun drop again as he clumsily bent at the waist, because she realized what he was doing. He was smelling her tea.

That night, she slept lightly with all the lodge's doors and windows locked and barricaded, a flashlight and her loaded pistol on the bedside.

The next morning, she woke up and realized the stiff hadn't beaten his way into the lodge.

Charlotte got up and did what she hadn't done for a long time; looked at herself in the master bedroom's oval mirror. When had she gotten *old*? Granted, she'd been living hard for a long time, but still...

She pulled her fine, grey-streaked, waist-length hair into a loose ponytail with a bit of string so she didn't look quite so much like a slob, then put on jeans and a sweater. When was the last time she had done a wash?

Her gun in her belt holster, she went downstairs and checked on the stiff through the kitchen window.

He was still on the porch, standing. Stiffs rarely sat or lay down for some reason. They didn't sleep either, but sometimes they just stayed in one place until they saw a living human.

Charlotte pulled an MRE pack out of one of cartons that filled the pantry to the roof, and ate breakfast while watching the stiff through the window.

"So, what do I do with you?" she said to the stiff outside, who shuffled back and forth across the porch. For a moment she wondered if he had reverted to instinct, but he still looked at her through the window.

There were a lot of things she could do. Leave him out there until she was absolutely sure he was safe. Leave him out there until he went away. Or just shoot him. Charlotte hadn't survived this long without being careful.

No, that wasn't quite right. She had survived because she had accepted how the world had changed, and adapted. If it changed again, she would adapt to that too.

Charlotte got up and went out the front door.

Charlotte put on surgical gloves and used scissors to cut away his ragged shirt and pants.

"Well, at least you've got all your parts," she said, eyeing his naked body. She poured a bucket of lukewarm water over him, noting that he didn't react at all to it. She roughly scrubbed him with a sponge, washing away accumulated years of dirt and grime,

Max's skin wasn't the mottled, rotting grey of a stiff, just pale and oddly tough-looking, like cooked meat. Patches of his skin over his throat and stomach looked closer to living human colour and texture.

"What *are* you?" Charlotte asked, to no answer. The most plausible theory she had heard about stiffs was that they were infected with something that repaired dead tissue, just enough to keep the victim moving around and infecting other people. Maybe somehow the infection kept repairing, very slowly, over years, until other human abilities returned?

Charlotte squinted, inching closer than she intended. He didn't have a stiff's rancid meat scent, but he didn't smell like an unwashed human either.

Max looked down at her studying him, his only movement in minutes.

Gingerly, she poked her latex-covered finger against the new flesh patch over the left side of his throat. Up close, it looked a little like the shape of a human bite mark, common on people attacked by stiffs; they usually went for the throat or stomach.

She had spent years avoiding and fighting stiffs, but there had been narrow escapes when she had felt them reaching for her, cold, twisted hands pawing at her with jerky movements. Those touches haunted her, making her wake suddenly in the night and reach for her gun. She had never been this close to a stiff without it being a life-

or-death struggle.

Under her hand, she felt a faint, slow pulse.

Something like a sob escaped her. Before she quite knew what she was doing, Charlotte wrapped her other arm around him and pulled herself close to him, mashing her body against his cold, still, naked body, pressing her mouth up to his throat the way some stiff must have bitten him ages ago.

He did nothing, did not come erect, nor hold her, nor kiss her back, he did not touch her at all. She might as well hump a corpse.

What the fuck am I doing? She shoved him away, wanting to rip her own contaminated skin off. Not taking her eyes off him, she retreated back into the lodge.

Charlotte slept even worse that night, with the lodge locked up tight again.

He came to her anyway, standing over her in her bed. She stared up at him, not moving, naked and still. His cold, solid mass covered her entire body, pressing her into the mattress. His teeth tore into her flesh without pain, peeling away her skin and muscle. The cool air caressed her internal organs as she bathed in her own warm blood.

The infection seeped through her being like black ink through white silk, eradicating all fear, all guilt, all pain, the seductiveness of *not caring*. Had all the billions of others fought against that and failed — ?

Charlotte jerked awake in the light of dawn, grabbed her pistol off the bedside and aimed it at nothing. Heart hammering against her ribs, she realized she was alone. She got up and crept down to the ground floor, gun at the ready. The doors were all still locked and barricaded, and Max was still on the porch.

"Shar-ut?" Max asked, looking at her.

She hid her gun behind her back. "Nothing. I'm just checking. Go back to sleep... or whatever."

Shivering with spent adrenalin, Charlotte splashed some cold water from the cooler on her face. What the hell was the matter with her?

The answer came to her. An old friend, whom Charlotte had seen dragged out of their car by undead hands a few days after the first outbreak, had been terrified of HIV, so scared that his fear wrapped around and became a strange kind of fascination. Even though he played safe and got tested every month, he was obsessed with HIV+ men, so much so that he'd try to date them and talked to her about "gift-givers".

It was fear, Charlotte decided. Live in fear of something for long enough and your mind would start eroticizing it just for relief, process the arousal as lust instead of terror.

That morning, Charlotte marched out to see Max, still standing on the porch. "Turn around," she commanded.

After a moment he did, facing the window into the kitchen. She could see the reflection of their faces as she stepped up behind him. He had that same blank look, while she looked grim.

She pulled her survival knife out of her gun belt's sheath, sharp steel hissing against old leather. Generally, if you were close enough to a stiff to use a knife, you had already made a huge mistake, and knives were pretty useless against stiffs anyway.

From behind, he looked more like just another stiff, except for those weird regenerated patches.

"Let's see how alive you are." She ran the point of her knife down his back, not hard enough to cut but enough to feel. But there was no response, not the slightest twitch. Was he numb all the way through?

She tried harder, this time cutting diagonally across his upper back. Still nothing. She might as well have cut a wax dummy. If he had turned and attacked her, she could have *understood* that, but this total lack of response was maddening. "Do you feel this?"

"Feel...?" he said. Something oozed out of the wound, thicker and darker than blood should be.

Her lips curled up from her teeth as she cut deeper. Some of the survivor groups Charlotte had joined captured lone stiffs and toyed with them, chopping off bits or using them for target practice, trying to see how much injury they could take before they stopped slavering

147

after humans. Charlotte didn't participate, but she didn't object much either, and she watched, compelled by the same fascination, trying to understand something that looked like a person but wasn't. What was clear was that stiffs didn't feel anything, not pain, but not hunger or thirst either. They were more like insects than humans or even animals.

"God damn it, do you feel anything?" Almost shaking with frustration and disappointment, she kicked at his legs. He stumbled forward and bumped against the lodge's wall, then turned around to look at her.

By instinct she dropped the knife and reached for her gun, and she was a hair's breadth away from gunning him down before she saw he wasn't attacking her. He looked hurt, she realized, not just frightened but confused, betrayed. She looked away, and caught her own reflection in the window, her own face distorted with cruel rage.

She took a few steps away from him, feeling sick of herself, sick of the world she had been cursed to survive in. They just stood there for a while, her as still as him, the only sounds the rustling of trees in the forest.

"I'm sorry, Max," she said at last. "I didn't hurt you... but I wronged you."

"Hurt... here," he said, brushing one clenched hand against his stomach.

"You're hungry?" She knew stiffs would bite and tear into living people, but that wasn't truly to eat, just to spread their infection; a pathetic imitation of human desire. Stiffs just kept going, without food or water, in defiance of all reason. "Wait here."

Charlotte dug the crackers out of an MRE packet and put them on the porch bannister between them. Max ate like he had never done it before, crumbs falling out of his open mouth. He swallowed, with a sound like the food being stuffed down a thin, dry tube.

Charlotte pulled the key off the belt ring and unlocked the door. "Here, you'd better come inside. Get you some clothes."

Still chewing the crackers, Max followed her into the lodge.

Charlotte still kept her pistol in her belt holster, but she wasn't quite so on edge when she took Max's vitals in the lodge's kitchen. "Pulse at rest, 40 beats per minute. Body temperature, 26 degrees Celsius. Both better than yesterday," she said, writing it down in a notebook next to the records for the past month. "Keep this up and you're going to be a real boy."

"Yes, Charlotte." Max now wore a pair of sweat pants and a t-shirt Charlotte had scrounged from the lodge. She'd also cut away the lank hair and a fresh crop of dark hair had grown in. His eyes were more focussed, with visible brown in the irises, and he moved a little more smoothly. "I want that." After listening to her talk and read to him, he spoke much more fluently.

Charlotte smiled and patted him on the shoulder, surprised at how casually she touched him now. Even so, when she felt a tug on her sleeve, she spun around, one hand on her holster. "What?"

"Look." Max slowly raised his arm at the kitchen window. She looked outside. Another stiff shuffled towards the cabin. This one had gotten through the fence without getting tangled.

"Max, stay inside." Charlotte drew her pistol, winced as she pulled back the slide with her bad hand, and headed outside.

After locking the front door, she ran to intercept the stiff.

It— *she* wore a torn, faded and stained pair of work coveralls, and her feet were bare. Long dark hair matted into dreadlocks dangled over her face. Like Max, she wasn't missing any parts.

Charlotte hesitated and kept her pistol pointed at the sky. Sure, there was Max, but he might be a one-in-a-billion fluke, and this stiff might be just like every other stiff in the world, a mindless thing that would rip her to shreds and infect her.

"Huh... heh..." she said, bare feet dragging across the grass.

Charlotte's heart hammered in her chest as the stiff shuffled closer, arms outstretched. She aimed between the cloudy white eyes and put her finger on the trigger, every instinct screaming at her to destroy this thing before it could touch her.

"...he-help..."

Charlotte let out a breath, eased her finger off the trigger and pointed the gun at the ground, almost dizzy with relief. "Yes, I'll help you."

The stiff stopped and seemed to be listening, her arms at her sides. Charlotte could see an embroidered name patch on her coveralls. "'Jamie,'" she read. "Your name is Jamie. I'm Charlotte."

"Hey, Max," she said over her shoulder. "It's a girl."

Chapter 2

The Body Electric

Now that Charlotte knew what to expect, she could help Jamie develop like Max.

Jamie rapidly caught up with Max in terms of speaking and coordination. She started eating sooner, and was a little ahead of him in intelligence. She even learned to say "Charlotte" properly before he had.

Part of what she was doing was teaching and part was her reminding them of what had been lost in the years of wandering around as stiffs. They did retain certain bits of knowledge from when they were alive, but nothing specific like their names or where they came from. Mercifully, she didn't have to toilet train them.

"*'Cause this is thrill-ah, thrill-ah night –* " sang the long-dead pop star on the lodge's stereo.

"One, two, three, four!" Charlotte commanded, facing Max and Jamie in the lodge's biggest room. "Claws left, claws right, claws walk, seven, eight."

The two ex-stiffs followed along with her, doing the steps and gestures as she had shown them.

"*'Cause I can thrill you more than any ghost would ever dare try –* "

"Shoulder lean, hip thrust, five, six, Jamie, you're a little behind, one, two..."

After a week of nightly dance routines, Max and Jamie stopped bumping into each other, and moved more fluidly, with better balance and coordination. Instead of just standing as still as mannequins most of the time, they moved like people, with posture and fidgeting and all of that. Charlotte could have done it with regular exercises, but why not have some fun with it?

The track ended in maniacal laughter, and the three of them moved the furniture back around the fireplace.

Max and Jamie sat on the couch, while Charlotte settled into the rocking chair and picked one of the lodge's assortment of books off the shelf.

This was part of the program too. Every night, she read to them. Though she knew they could only understand a tiny fraction of it, just hearing the words fascinated them. She guessed that the more they used a capacity, the better it got. The more they moved, the more agile and balanced they became. The more she talked to them, the more they could talk.

She had never been much for reading before, and certainly not poetry. But she liked reading Walt Whitman's *Leaves of Grass*, just for the way it felt to say the lines.

> *"I have perceiv'd that to be with those I like is enough,*
> *To stop in company with the rest at evening is enough,*
> *To be surrounded by beautiful, curious, breathing, laughing flesh is*
> *   enough,*
> *To pass among them or touch any one, or rest my arm ever so lightly*
> *round his or her neck for a moment, what is this then?*
> *I do not ask any more delight, I swim in it as in a sea."*

Charlotte choked up and stopped. She tried to control herself, especially in front of them, but it got out anyway. "All that's gone. Nothing left but stiffs. Billions of lumps of ugly, stupid, twitching, rotting meat that don't even know they're dead. And me. I get to see all of it. The last human being alive. The last soul."

She wanted to throw the book into the fire, burn it, burn the lodge and everything else that could possibly remind her of what was gone, walk out the front door and keep walking until she found a stiff and let it do the only thing it did. Just end it. What did it matter?

Max and Jamie just watched her, as they always did, learning from everything they saw her do.

I have responsibilities now. "I need..." Charlotte said, choked. "I'll be back in a minute."

In the kitchen, she splashed cold water on her face. There were moments when it all got to her. Now, she was glad she had thrown out all the liquor last year.

Sniffling a bit, she walked back to the living room, wondering why she didn't want to cry in front of them.

She stopped at the doorway, where she could see Max and Jamie on the couch, facing the fire, away from her. In the red-gold light of the crackling fire, their skins looked less pallid, more human. They used to sit like dolls a giant child had forgotten, unnaturally still, but now they sat right next to each other, arms just touching.

Max lifted his arm up slowly and put it across Jamie's shoulders. After a moment, Jamie's hand inched forward until it rested on his thigh.

Charlotte held her breath as she watched. Was this what people felt when the pandas in zoos finally started mating?

Max reached up with one hand and touched Jamie's face, cool skin on cool skin, hesitant as trying to touch a butterfly's wing.

If they had been sitting close to the fire for a while, Charlotte thought, they'd feel warmer, more like a living person. She remembered what it was like, years ago, to touch someone else without fear, the men and women who had shared her bed.

They were face to face now, nuzzling like they wanted to kiss but had forgotten how. Max's hand, his fingers rigid and clumsy, bumped against Jamie's ear. Charlotte wanted to grab his hand and guide it through a caress, teach him how stroke her hair, rub her neck. *Here, like this.*

Watching them, she felt like something inside her was melting, flowing again. Her good hand slipped down the front of her pants, at first just to adjust her damp panties, but she stayed there, rubbing herself.

Max and Jamie kept fumbling at each other, struggling to relearn how to give and receive touch. The floorboards creaked under her feet. As one, Max and Jamie looked up, saw her watching and twitched away from each other.

Oh great, I just taught them shame. Charlotte pulled her hand out of her pants and cleared her throat. "Okay, where were we?" She got back in the rocking chair and picked up the book. *"There is something in staying close to men and women...."*

After an afternoon of checking her game traps, Charlotte carried a couple of rabbits back to the lodge. Max and Jamie were working at the woodpile, Max splitting logs with an axe and Jamie stacking them. They did good work; in fact, sometimes she had to tell them to stop, as they didn't get tired. That was the problem. They still didn't quite act like *people* yet, and their development had plateaued for the past couple of weeks.

"Mom's home," she began to say, but bit it down. That set up uncomfortable comparisons for her.

"Hello, Charlotte," they said in slightly flat unison.

Charlotte had to admit that she had qualms about what she was planning. With their consent, she had pricked their fingers and seen that they had what appeared to be human blood now. They even smelled like regular people, so she assumed that they weren't infectious any more.

But that was just one of the reasons why she hesitated. Max and Jamie were becoming more alive, but they weren't all there yet. They were a little like children, or maybe more like mental patients. Could they consent? Would they be so eager to please her that she could push them beyond what they were ready for? Did she need to restrain herself for their sake?

Then again, who the hell knew what morality was any more? She might very well be the only living human left in the world, the only person who remotely cared. This might be the only way they could continue to develop, the only way the human race could survive.

Or maybe, after years of being alone, she just needed to touch somebody else.

Charlotte tried to find something "nice" in her clothing, but everything was worn-out, rugged or both. Finally, she found a large piece of thin, floral print cloth and wrapped it around herself with the knot at her neck, sarong-dress style. All she had for jewellery was a heart-shaped pendant she had somehow hung onto.

She looked at herself in the mirror; not bad, all things considered. She had been a bit vain, once, but years of hard living had worn that away. Still, now that she looked at her grey-streaked hair, thin body, lined face and less-than-perky breasts, she felt like she was letting them down.

She made them a special dinner on the wood stove, cedar-grilled venison with wild rice and mushrooms, followed by the last of the canned peaches. They devoured it, not just out of hunger but an appetite for new tastes, new sensations. They barely listened when she reminded them of table manners. What was that like, she wondered, to have a whole sense re-awaken? Maybe something like having new people to talk to after being alone for years.

After dinner and washing up, Charlotte broke routine and led them up to the master bedroom on the second floor. Max and Jamie looked around with what she had learned was curiosity. This was the first time she let them in here; she had them sleep in the downstairs bedrooms.

She sat on the edge of the big bed in the cabin's master bedroom, picking at the comforter. This wasn't her first time with a woman; she'd waffled between identifying as bi and straight. This wasn't even her first threesome. But this was unknown territory for everybody. "Okay, I've seen you touching each other. That's a good thing. What you need to know is, there's more. The most important thing is, if you don't want to do this, you don't have to. If anybody at any time says, 'stop,' you have to stop. Understand?"

"Yes, Charlotte," they said again in that slightly creepy unison.

She stood up. "This is how people show they like each other," she explained as she undid the knot of her sarong and let it fall. She had to help them get undressed, their clumsy fingers too slow for her.

With light touches, she moved them around so they were facing each other. Their skins were warmer under her hands than she expected, though still cool, like they had just come in from the cold.

"Kissing is a good way to start." She had to get up on her toes and gently pull Max's head down just so their lips could touch, but his mouth didn't respond to her. It was weird, not just the difference in their bodies, but he literally had no idea how to kiss. "Like you're eating something delicious." Her choice of words brought up unpleasant memories, but Max seemed to get it. After bumping teeth once, their lips caressed each other.

Oops, don't play favourites. "Here, Jamie," she said, pulling her close and doing the same. As in other things, she was a quicker student. Before long, she turned her attentions to Max.

Charlotte smiled in appreciation as her charges kissed and embraced, remembering her own fumbling first kiss in the music room after school. Their hands roamed over each other. She put her hand over Max's, guiding him in stroking up Jamie's side and cupping her breast, then moved Jamie's hand to stroke his back and buttocks. They grew less hesitant and more energetic with each touch.

She pulled them onto the bed, helping them lie side by side in a position that wasn't uncomfortable. They almost forgot she was there as they explored each other, but Charlotte didn't mind. This was about them, not her. She lounged on the edge of the bed, the mattress creaking beneath them, happy to throw in a pinch here or a stroke there with her good hand while they explored each other. Whether they were remembering some forgotten response or learning it all brand new, she didn't care. To see them acting with desire and passion, giving and receiving pleasure, after being numb and dead for years, was the most beautiful thing she had seen in her life.

Maybe it was her imagination, but as they touched, every part of them grew warmer, more supple, more alive. Running her fingers through the wetness between Jamie's legs, or wrapping her fingers around Max's firm cock, was witnessing a minor miracle.

"Here, let's try something." Charlotte rested Jamie's head in her lap and moved Max's hand to her vulva. "Like this. Find the way she likes best." Her fingers and Max's slipped around and between Jamie's wet inner lips, searching for the right pressure and rhythm.

As Charlotte helped him guide Jamie towards climax, something unexpected happened. Jamie's pants and sighs kept growing stronger until she had what looked more like a seizure than an orgasm, every muscle convulsing. Jamie looked like someone waking up from a nightmare, eyes wide and searching the room, her hands clutching at them in panic. "Shh, you're okay." Charlotte held Jamie close and kissed her forehead. "You're better than okay." Max held her tight too, kissing her throat with a strange mix of passion and brotherly concern.

Under Charlotte's care, Jamie calmed down, and kept looking around, far more alert and curious than before. "It's.... everything's different."

With newfound eagerness, she slipped out of Charlotte's embrace and reached for Max, almost attacking him. "You have to see, there's more — " She kissed Max and grabbed for his crotch, so rough that he drew away.

"Hey, slow down there a little." Charlotte actually had to pull her back from him. "It's not a gear shift." She moved around to kneel behind Max so she could show Jamie how to stroke him.

When Max came, spurting across Jamie's thigh, he had the same seizure-like reaction, and Charlotte was careful to keep him grounded with touch. "Just ride it out, Max, it'll be okay."

Max's breathing slowed back to normal. He looked around, taking in the room and them, as if he had never seen them before. "Yes," he said, holding Jamie tight as Charlotte hugged him from behind, "there's more." Charlotte could only guess that the arousal and orgasm awoke some numbed capacity in them. Their eyes were far more aware and focussed, in the way they looked at her and each other.

They could *know*, now, Charlotte thought, melancholy tainting her pleasure. They could understand what had happened to them and the world, how much had been lost. But she would help them through that when the time came. For now, this was a triumph of desire over reflex.

"C'mere, you two." She pulled the comforter over them, cuddling in between them.

In the lodge's master bedroom, Charlotte spooned into Max's embrace, cooing as he kissed and nibbled her ears and cupped her breasts. Jamie lay between Charlotte's spread legs, her tongue lapping at Charlotte's clit like a kitten with a saucer of cream.

Every day, their flesh was just a little warmer and softer, their fingers and lips and tongues on her body more agile. They talked like people, not robots. She had even caught them *arguing* with each other, had to settle disputes.

"Just there, like that—" Charlotte panted, rubbing Jamie's soft, newly grown hair with her good hand. "Just a little more and I'll—"

The jangling cans outside made her arousal collapse. For a moment, she hoped it was just a coyote or something and she could ignore it, but she knew better. She wriggled out of their embrace, despite their protests, padded out onto the balcony, grabbed the binoculars and scanned the perimeter.

"Motherfuckers..." Charlotte said, feeling a chill that had nothing to do with her nudity. A mob of thirteen stiffs were tearing their way through the perimeter fence, yanking the barbed wire out of the stakes and tangling it around their limbs.

She had planned for a large group attacking the lodge; stay on the balcony and pick them off one by one with rifle fire. But she remembered what had changed; some, or even all of them could be like Max and Jamie. She couldn't just put them down.

"Motherfuckers," Jamie repeated, followed by Max, who then went back to nibbling on Jamie's nipples.

"Watch your mouth," Charlotte said as she pulled on her bathrobe. Max and Jamie had started to change presumably before they saw another human being, yet the other stiffs hadn't turned on them. But now they had changed so much, would the stiffs attack them? She couldn't take the risk. "Stay here, both of you!"

They stopped making out and watched her as she hurried downstairs.

They're afraid, Charlotte marvelled, as she stepped into her gumboots. She grabbed the rifle off the gun rack, then slung the shotgun over her shoulder as a backup.

After checking the front door peep hole, she cranked the door open, stepped out and locked the door behind her. Outside, she could smell the stiffs from here, that godawful reek that was more of a taste in the air. She flicked the rifle's safety off and crept around the porch, headed for the corner of the house.

There they were. The baker's dozen of stiffs were tangled up in bits of the barbed wire fence and their own entrails, sliding out of slashed stomach cavities, yet somehow they could still move forwards. Charlotte thought of the picture she had seen as a girl of a rat king, a swarm of rats with their tails tangled together. She'd had nightmares about that for months afterwards. Could some of the bodies in this thing be coming back to life? "Can you hear me?" she shouted.

Insect-like reflex made the amalgamated stiffs shamble towards her, the barbed wire lacerating their dead grey flesh open with each step.

"If you can understand me, say something! Stop!" Her own instincts made Charlotte shoulder her rifle, her finger twitching on the trigger. The smell crawled into her nose, making her gag.

The stiff-horde just kept creeping closer, each idiotic component walking independently, some hopelessly tangled and being dragged along, mangled arms and legs flailing.

"Last chance—" she shouted.

Nothing resembling speech, just an inarticulate, composite groan from the stiffs.

Sorry. She swallowed down bile, switched the rifle to single-fire and took aim. *Head shot, always the head.*

One stiff's head exploded, then another, each slowing it down a little more. But it was taking too long. Charlotte switched to full auto and sprayed the mob, aiming low and hoping for a mobility kill to buy time. Stiff leg bones splintered, but kept working, mindlessly dragging the amalgam towards the closest uninfected human. Charlotte.

After two bursts, something *clunked* inside the rifle's mechanism when she pulled the trigger. *Shit!* No time to clear the jam. Back-pedalling, she dropped the rifle and brought up the shotgun. *Only five shells; two to spare.* Her bad hand burned as she pumped the slide and took aim.

The pile of rotting flesh and barbed wire shambled forward, arms twisted like driftwood reaching for her, black-toothed mouths open and drooling.

Charlotte picked off the head of the foremost stiff, biting down a yelp at her left hand's pain as she pumped the slide and fired again, getting rid of the next to last one.

It wasn't just her arthritic hand, her entire left side throbbed with pain like a searing hot blanket. *Shit...* Charlotte thought as she dropped to one knee. *My heart...* She desperately tried to stay up, then got dizzy and crumpled to the ground.

She gritted through the pain. The stiffs crept closer, still faster than she could crawl away to the safety of the lodge. She thrashed her right arm and leg, trying to move.

Hands grabbed at her, pulled at her. She struggled, panicked at the thought of becoming one of *them*, the dead things that claimed this planet in the mockery of humanity. They were too strong and too many and all she could hope was that her own heart killed her before they did... *Who'll look after Max and Jamie?*

Wait, those were *warm* hands.

"We're coming to get you, Charlotte."

Charlotte looked up into Max's face as he picked her up, easily carrying her in his arms.

She managed to turn her head. Jamie, still naked like Max, picked up the shotgun and shot at the last of the stiffs, but she had no idea how to compensate for the recoil. Two shots went wild and the one last active stiff still dragged the rest of them with it. Finally, Jamie just shoved the barrel right into the last stiff's slack, black-drooling mouth and fired. The stiff's head burst into grey muck.

"Clever girl," Charlotte muttered through the pain.

As she asked, Max carried her to the ground floor bathroom, where she got the nitroglycerin tablet out of the emergency kit and put it under her tongue. The relief was immediate.

"Put me down, gently," she said. "Jamie, go lock the front door like I showed you." She hadn't lived this long without being careful.

Max gently put her down on the floor. She sagged there, shivering with spent adrenalin.

Jamie came back and said, "Sorry."

"What for?"

"You told us to stay inside," Max explained.

Charlotte almost laughed. "Help me up, will you?"

Max half-carried her into the master bedroom, where they helped her back into bed.

"Read to us, please." Max handed her the book on the bedside.

They crawled under the covers on either side of her, and she could feel their breathing, their beating hearts, their warm skins. They thought and felt and cared. They even disobeyed orders to save her. She opened the book at random and read:

> "I sing the body electric,
> The armies of those I love engirth me and I engirth them,
> They will not let me off till I go with them, respond to them,
> And discorrupt them, and charge them full with the charge of the
>   soul."

She spent the rest of the summer teaching Max and Jamie everything she could; how to shoot, how to drive and fix the pickup, how to recognize safe food and water, how to find stores and hospitals and libraries, how to read. When the leaves started turning brown, she realized there wasn't anything else she could tell them and she'd have to trust in their own intelligence.

They stood in a triangle next to the truck, packed with as many supplies, guns and books as could fit. Max and Jamie had grown more alive every day, their faces expressive. Charlotte thought they looked like children trying to be brave. They still didn't remember anything from their former lives; everything was brand new for them.

Charlotte didn't know why the world had ended, why the stiffs consumed the human race, why she had survived when billions had not. She didn't know why Max and Jamie had become human again, but she could live with that mystery. Charlotte didn't believe in God or destiny or anything else really, even before the stiffs, but when she looked at her newly-reborn charges, moving and eating and talking and loving again because of her care, she felt her life had... not purpose, exactly, but meaning.

"We want you to come with us," Jamie said.

Charlotte shook her head. "I'd slow you down." Ever since that day when the stiffs attacked, she hadn't been the same. She got tired too easily, and she had to admit to herself she was in no shape for life on the road.

"You helped us," said Max.

"Yes, and you helped me."

They looked at each other, confused. "I don't understand," said Max.

"It's okay. You will someday, and that's what's important." There was so much she wanted to say to them. *Keep it simple*, she thought. She grasped their hands and pressed them together, wincing when the arthritis in both of her hands burned, but the contact was a blessing. "There must be others like you out there. Look for them. Help them, the way I helped you."

"Yes, Charlotte," they said in unison.

"What else...?" She felt like she was writing down new commandments. "Um, look after each other. Treat people the way they want to be treated."

"Yes, Charlotte," they said again.

She kissed them both quickly, then forced herself to let go of their hands. "You have to go now." The broken contact felt like an amputation. "You have to *go!*"

She turned and walked back to the lodge, forcing herself not to look back or cry. As she closed the door behind her, she heard the truck engine start.

Charlotte climbed the stairs to the master bedroom, something more difficult each day. On the balcony, she watched them drive away.

They were at the gate now. She watched them get out, open it, drive the pickup through and shut it behind them. The truck rolled down the dirt road and disappeared into the forest, into the world.

She climbed into bed and pulled the down comforter over her tired body. She could rest now.

If you enjoyed this story, you can discuss it with other readers and the author at *The Charge of the Soul* story page at
http://forbiddenfiction.com/library/story/PT1-1.000038.

About the Authors

Claryssa Berg is a Norwegian writer of smutty fairy tales of various kinds, who has been published in English since 2004. When she is not twisting myths and ravaging fairy tales, she lives a quiet life in a smallish city in the middle of Norway, together with her son and her cat.

Ruth Black is an ex-journalist who turned to writing fiction in her spare time, and found she enjoyed it much more than reporting the local news. She now writes lots of different kinds of stories and novels under various pseudonyms. She is a practicing Pagan. She lives in Scotland with her husband, two cats and a broomstick.

Theda Black was born in the South, and moved as a young adult on a whim to Philly (with two cats, a hamster, a TV set and her best friend, all packed into a tiny Mazda GLC). It was a great adventure, and Theda ended up staying a couple of years before heading home to Tennessee again, where she's been ever since. Theda likes horror, erotica, and GLBT stories, so that's what she writes.

Jane Potter is a student by day, a writer by night, and an avid tea-drinker at all hours. She has always been fascinated by the supernatural, and often combines her knowledge of various mythologies and lores with an interest in the darker side of the human experience. As a result, she writes the stories that she always wanted to read but could never talk about.

Ann Gimpel is a clinical psychologist, with a Jungian bent. Avocations include mountaineering, skiing, wilderness photography and, of course, writing. A lifelong aficionado of the unusual, she began writing speculative fiction a few years ago. Since then her short fiction has appeared in a number of webzines and anthologies and she has published two novels, *Psyche's Prophecy* and *Psyche's Search*. *Psyche's Promise*, last book in that series, is slated for release during the summer of 2012. A husband, grown children, grandchildren and three wolf hybrids round out her family.

E.E. Grey started to write fresh out of high school, but the hobby grew over time. Now Grey has completed six novel-length works and over three hundred short stories. When not writing, Grey likes to travel, having visited twenty countries already with several still on the list for the future.

Konrad Hartmann lives in Pennsylvania and is the following: a wannabe anthropologist/mineral collector, a nerd, a cat owner, a lurker of local flea markets, a gardener, a descendant of miners and railwaymen and liverymen and Swiss Mennonites, not Amish, recently a theremin-owner, a homebrewer, someone who writes in a basement and drinks cider, interested in dowsing and folk magic and Celto-Germanic history, a weirdo, inspired by Richard Shaver. Although Konrad's own writings sometimes give him pause, he feels that we must allow our unconscious to become conscious, though we may dread what comes of it, and though we may despair of what gives us pleasure.

Luna Lawrence lives near the ocean where she grew up. She's acquired some letters before and after her name, but they don't mean as much as the lessons she's learned wandering the world, from China to Guatemala. Luna writes fantasy and mystery as well.

Annabeth Leong found relief in erotica. Reading others' stories opened up a world of freedom and exploration. Writing it increased the thrill. Since her first published story in 2009, she has written for anthologies by Cleis Press, Ravenous Romance, Coming Together, and Circlet. Her work has appeared online at Every Night Erotica and Oysters and Chocolate. She is pleased to participate in Forbidden Fiction's Special Collections. Besides freedom of speech, Annabeth loves shoes, stockings, cooking, and attending concerts--probably in that order. She lives in Providence, Rhode Island.

Kailin Morgan has always been an avid reader. She discovered goth and industrial music and vampires and werewolves at about the same time. As part of the alternative subculture, she has always been open to different fashions, tattoos and piercings and self-expression. She rediscovered the love of writing through fan-fiction and has since quickly become addicted to the thrill of discovering new characters. Although most of her writing is m/m, she also loves writing strong female characters. Her writing tends towards fantasy, dealing with gods and monsters, but she loves to place them into everyday settings and see what happens. Now a slave to the muse, Kailin looks forward to spending many hours hiding from the Scottish weather, hunched over her laptop, typing feverishly whilst existing solely on caffeine.

Peter Tupper is a writer, journalist and historian in Vancouver, BC. His non-fiction has appeared in *Wired* magazine, the *Utne Reader*, *THIS* magazine, the *Tyee*, and more. His erotic fiction has appeared in several science fiction and fantasy anthologies, including the steampunk erotica story collection *The Innocent's Progress & Other Stories*.

About the Publisher

ForbiddenFiction.com is a publisher devoted to writing that breaks the boundaries of original erotic fiction. Our stories combine intense sexuality with quality writing. Stories at ForbiddenFiction.com not only arouse readers through sensations, but also engage them emotionally and mentally through storytelling as well-crafted as the sex is hot.

ForbiddenFiction.com is also designed to be a social reading environment. You'll have fun even if just reading the latest post each day, yet you will have the chance for so much more. Readers and authors can be part of ongoing discussions of specific works and individual authors as well as more general topics.

Sign up for a FREE Membership today at ForbiddenFiction.com

www.ingramcontent.com/pod-product-compliance
Lightning Source LLC
Chambersburg PA
CBHW060740180626
46819CB00001B/54